THE LAST

SUNSET

By Jason Summers

For my readers, who continue to inspire me to create.

Chapter One

She never guessed that morning that this would be her final day on earth. But as the day went on, and many of the dark thoughts and realisations of just what had happened over the last few years in her marriage came to light, she knew that she just couldn't take it anymore.

Her husband was away on another one of his so-called business trips, which she knew now were mostly just thinly veiled excuses for him to go and spend time with his latest version of twenty-something year old blonde assistants. She looked at her last message she had typed out to him a few hours earlier, and noted that it had been read, with no reply incoming. She sipped from her wine glass and looked over to the top of her island bench; the bottle on it was almost empty, the second for the night, and she could feel the effects of the toxic dose of Valium and Oxycodone she had taken beginning to take hold.

She wanted it to be grisly. She wanted him to see. To see the pain and hurt that he had caused her over these years. She chuckled at herself at just how stupid it all was. Her therapist, many times, had tried to give her context on her depression, to try and alleviate the pain and dark thoughts. But she was just like everyone else. Write the prescriptions. Give the pills. Next. She got up from her couch in the lounge room with wine glass in hand and steadied herself to look around her home one last time. The home was a beautiful early century federation property, which had been heritage listed many years earlier. She had commissioned massive renovations, and the rear of the property was a modern masterpiece, with a mixture of Italian granite, polished concrete and pastel-coloured tones. She had done all of the interior decorating in the home; she had put her blood, sweat and tears into turning the dilapidated home into a beautiful piece of architecture, and all she got was a gruff, 'Thanks,' at the end of it all.

The hallway to the front of the home was long and narrow and was a forgotten time capsule of the old federation home from back in its heyday. Along it ran a pale green Afghan carpet runner which spanned nearly ten metres. The hallway started at the front door and ended at the entrance of the cavernous extension, which was built off the rear of the home. Photo frames adorned both sides of the hallway, and she walked silently along it, and looked at each image like she was viewing each milestone in her life for the final time. The photos at the front door were in the early days. The courtship and the fun. The other couples, pre-kids and pre-commitments, when everyone had time and money and freedom to do whatever they wanted. Now, she mourned that life, as her friends got older and had children, and slowly moved away from her and into their new lives. And she mourned the children that she never had, and never could have.

Further down the hallway in the middle section, the photos began to change into a couple heading into their early 30s who had money to burn. Beautiful tropical beaches, sun tanned skin, low body fat. Alpine ranges, sunburnt faces and white smiles on the ski slopes. A couple who had all the money, all the time, and no burden on them, a simpler time. As that couple got closer to present day, the photos changed again, and from where she stood, she couldn't find a single photo where that happy couple at the beginning were even in the same images together. Golf trips, girls' trips, photos of their dog. All a mish mash of singular occasions that they deemed were worthy of the wall. And in hindsight, a true reflection of where their marriage had headed.

She walked down the length of the hallway to the garage door and made her way inside. Her car sat in solitude in the space, and she made her way behind it to the shelving units and shuffled through various crates until she found what she was looking for. The rope she held in her hands was one she had used before. She remembered a trip to Tasmania where she had used that same rope to tie a canoe she had hired up to a post. She remembered using it as a lead for her bulldog, Remi, on a camping trip when she had forgotten her lead. She looked down at it, and let the fibres run through her hands. It was thick and sturdy and would do the job perfectly.

A noise startled her coming from the garage doorway, and she wasn't surprised to see Remi standing curiously in the opening. She was her ever-watchful eye, her security guard, and her companion. As the little dog watched her, she slowly began to wonder whether she was making the right decision. There was no one on this earth she cared about more than that little dog, and she wondered whether Spencer would keep her. He'd never seemed to like her. But it was her time. And she knew she needed to make a selfish decision, the ultimate sacrifice.

'Hey girl,' she said, as she bent down and scratched the dog under the chin. Remi's ears shot back instinctively, grateful for her mother's love. She stood up and wiped the tears from her eyes as she walked back down the hallway, and could feel Remi's cheek bumping against her left calf muscle as she walked by her side for the final time.

The weather was still, the sky clear, and the temperature was in the early 20s. A perfect spring night on the verge of summer. She could see the sun lowering near the horizon through her back door, and as she stood near the opening, she tried to mentally prepare herself. She turned back and tipped the final remnants of wine into her glass, and drank the few mouthfuls, hoping the liquid courage would help her do what she needed to do. As she reached with the glass to place it back on the bench, the drugs had begun to affect her coordination, and the glass balanced for a moment, and then tipped and hit the floor with a sudden smash, flicking the remnants of red wine up onto the pristine gloss white cabinetry. She left it; it wasn't her problem anymore. She turned back for the door, slid it open, and stepped out onto the back deck.

The setting was serene, the pool to the left was heated to a perfect temperature and lit up with LED lights for the nighttime swims they had had in happier times. The deck and outdoor kitchen, now empty, where she and her husband had entertained friends and family. The rolling grass and gardens of their beautiful home, all designed by herself with help from a prominent Sydney landscape architect. And finally, the Oak tree. The Oak tree that she had got married under, the Oak tree that she had spent days lounging under as a newlywed, the Oak tree she had raised and trained Remi her companion under, and finally the Oak tree where she would end her life.

The tree was huge, and from all accounts, over two hundred years old. The trunk was over a metre round, and the branches were gnarled and twisted from surviving the wild weather of all of those years. Being spring, tiny sprays of yellow and green flowers had bloomed all over, and during the day she marvelled at the beauty of it. The tree was a constant. People, buildings, even other vegetation came and went. The Oak outlasted all. And she knew was about to outlast her own life.

She had gone on YouTube earlier in the week, and it was almost like her mind had begun preparation long before her heart had. She had searched how to tie a noose; and she had watched the videos, and was surprised now how easily she managed to tie the elaborate knot with no instructions. It was like death knew that it was her time. She looked up to one of the thick sturdy branches and managed to throw the rope up over it, then pulled the other end through the loop. As the rope began to tighten, she realised her fault almost immediately; the rope was much too short for how high the Oak branches were. She looked around and spotted her wrought iron garden bench and walked over to try and slide it closer to the trunk. She pulled it as hard as she could, but the hundred-year-old piece of garden furniture wouldn't budge.

She turned back to the tree and eyed the lowest branch around shoulder height. She would climb up and go from there. She walked close to the trunk, and with surprising athleticism, vaulted herself up to the shoulder high branch, and cursed herself as she scratched both of her forearms in the process. She wiped the blood off her left arm with the end of her t-shirt and stood on the thick branch in the silence. What would her friends think of her? How would she be remembered? She thought of Spencer in her final few minutes. Her husband, who she thought was her one true love, and the pain that he had caused her and others over the years.

The scene was still except for Remi, who watched her mother with curiosity from a safe distance. She looked out at her companion one last time, and once again wiped tears from her eyes. 'Bye Remi,' she said as she affixed the noose around her neck. She stepped forward, and her body fell toward the ground quickly, as the rope went taut. The violent snap of her neck was the last sound that went through her ears, and she brought both of her hands up to the noose around her neck as she tried to fight for her last few breaths. Her body swung and twitched for a few more seconds, until finally, her eyes, now bloodshot, remained transfixed on her last ever sunset.

Chapter Two

The river was long and straight, and Detective Sergeant Nick Vada stood on the edge of the bank and shielded the sunlight from his eyes. He was out west, in the middle of nowhere, around fifty kilometres from a little town called Coleambally, and was fairly sure he was wasting his time.

Nick had been sent out to help investigate the death of a farmer, a man named Leo Voltari, and sensed from the beginning that whatever had happened to the man had ties to the drug trade. His body had been found in the bush, around twenty kilometres from his farm in the thick scrubland, by a father and son on their annual camping trip from Sydney. It would be a camping trip that they would never forget. His body lay face first on the harsh earth, with the back of his head left an absolute mess. He hadn't made it in time to assess his body at the scene, but the crime scene services team, along with local detectives, had managed to write up an impressive report along with extensive photographs of the incident.

Nick watched the black shape moving slowly toward the edge of the riverbank and he walked down the jagged and eroded bank to meet it. The police diver soon emerged and trudged slowly out of the thick mud onto the bank. He pulled his eye mask up and rested it on his forehead, and with a swift press on the side of his mouthpiece, cleared the excess oxygen from his respirator.

Nick had worked with him before and remembered him distinctly from a job back in Sydney in the Hawkesbury River, where they searched for the remains of a missing woman, after an anonymous phone tip-off. He was nearly his height, and underneath his thick rubber diving suit had a shock of green dyed hair, to go along with the coloured tattoos on his neck that he could see. 'Any luck?' he asked.

'Nothing. Can hardly see two feet in front of me. Visibilities very low.'

'Bugger. I thought for sure we might find something.'

The edge of the river was only a five hundred metre walk from where the body was found and an informant had told someone from their undercover division that apparently after the hit, the gun was disposed of in a nearby river. He thought that the retrieval of the weapon may have been an easy task, but watching the fast-flowing current of the Darling River, he wondered just how far a gun could move from where it was initially dropped? He made a note to try and speak with the undercover officer again to see if he could glean any further information. He knew it might make this search a whole lot easier.

The diver walked back to his truck, which was parked up at the end of the beaten path they had made through the rough bushland and grabbed another oxygen bottle from the back tray. He moved back down toward the riverbank as Nick watched and connected the fresh tank to his respirator.

'This is my last tank. I'll have one more go. If worse comes to worse, I may be able to get some of the other team here later next week. But looking at that current, we may be out of luck.'

Nick nodded in agreement. 'It's the snow melt. It's getting worse.'

The diver looked at him curiously. 'Yep, climate change and all that. You know the rivers well.'

'Yeah. Grew up on the Edward River.'

The diver pulled his mask back down and cleared his respirator again. 'Wish me luck.'

Nick watched the diver slowly wade into the dark brown water until he was just a line of bubbles coming to the water's surface. He looked past the water, at the riverbank on the opposite side, and the towering gumtrees all cut into the side of the banks. Years of erosion and manipulation of the water levels from the Murray-Darling basin scheme had killed many of the thriving river systems in the state, and he knew with how climate change was going, that many of the farmers who relied on the water to keep their crops alive may need to seriously look into potential alternative farming techniques if they wanted to survive in the future.

Standing in the silence, he felt a peace out on the riverbank that he never felt in the city, and the deathly quiet and stillness of the bush made him feel at ease. His recent promotion to the head of rural homicide within his elite Sydney homicide unit had been easy for his boss, Chief Inspector of homicide, Mark Johnson. It was cursory title really he knew, as he was mostly a one-man team, with the added support of Hattie Boyd, a tech analyst, and whatever local support could be afforded during each case. The one advantage with his role, and his notoriety on some of his recent cases, was that he had carte blanche in regard to budgeting and extra resources when needed with the powers to be. Most requests he asked for were granted immediately, and he felt proud to have that amount of freedom to make sure his job was done right.

The shrill of his mobile phone shattered the quiet stillness on the riverbank and he pulled it out of his pocket to see his girlfriend, Bec, ringing. 'Hello?'

Nick could tell by her ragged breathing that she was crying as she was trying to speak. 'Hey, hey, hey. Breathe, calm down, what's wrong?' he asked.

'It's. It's.. It's.. Emily,' she said through sobs.

Nick assumed she was speaking about Emily Hartford, her best friend. They had met when Bec worked back in Edithvale as a crime scene services officer a few years back and kept in touch as much as they possibly could, despite living at near opposite ends of the state. Emily still lived in Edithvale, and despite only meeting her once, he had liked her and enjoyed her company.

'What about Emily?' he asked.

'She's dead Nick.'

Nick stood on the riverbank in shock. She was only a few years older than Bec; he guessed early 40s, and he didn't remember hearing anything about her being sick. 'What happened?'

Nick heard Bec breathe in and out and then whimper. 'Suicide.'

Bec had told him of some of her mental health battles and now, thinking back, he should've thought of that first. 'Babe. I'm sorry. Is there anything I can do?'

'Can you get home? I need to go to Edithvale. I need to be there for Spencer.'

Nick thought of his caseload and how busy the last few months had been as he watched the diver's bubbles turning and beginning to head back toward the bank. He would need to speak with the chief and ask for temporary leave from this case. The local team seemed competent enough, and he was sure that they were going to struggle to find the killer. The people who committed execution style killings like this were always meticulous with planning. He knew their best chance of catching the killer was more likely to be through information from their informants they had in their narcotics division.

'Of course. Let me call the chief and call you back.'

The diver emerged from the water once again, but this time, as his head, then shoulders emerged from the dark water, Nick could see he was holding in his arm what was sure to be their murder weapon. Covered in mud and silt was a .22 calibre rifle which looked to be in good condition despite its short stay underwater. He was sure further testing would verify it as their murder weapon.

The diver put his mask on his head and smiled. 'Can't believe it. It was lodged under a tree root. We were bloody lucky.' Nick quickly placed on gloves and the diver passed the rifle over to him. 'Looks like it's only been under for a few days. I reckon this is it.'

After helping the diver pack up his tanks and gear, he placed the rifle into a special clear evidence bag from his boot that he used for weapons and jumped into his unmarked police car. He followed the taillights of the diver's truck through the thick scrub along the rutted dirt track, until they came to a clearing that they had turned off from the main road. The diver's window was down and as he turned to the right, towards Sydney, he gave him a wave before departing in that direction. Nick turned left to make the drive back to Coleambally to give the local detective the weapon, and eyed the signal reception for his phone in the cradle, waiting for it to get to two bars before he opened his contacts, to call the chief inspector.

The phone sound was loud through his Bluetooth speakers, and he turned the volume down slightly, not used to the noise again after the peace in the bush, as he waited for the Chief to answer.

'Afternoon. How's it going down there?' The chief asked.

'Good. The diver found a rifle. Got it bagged in the car.'

'Right. Does it look like our murder weapon?'

Nick indicated from the gravel road out onto the state highway, which ran from east to west across the state. 'It's only been in the water for a few days. So, unless some campers decided to offload their rifles right near our crime scene, I think we're in luck.'

There was silence at the end of the line, and he could hear the chief talking in the background. 'Sorry, busy here, that the reason for the call?' The chief asked.

'No. It's not. I'm going to need to take a few days if that works?'

There was silence again for a beat. 'Yeah, of course. What's wrong?'

'It's Bec, sir. Her best friend has passed away. Last night apparently.'

'Who's that?'

'Emily Hartford. From Edithvale.'

'Hartford. Hartford. Any relation to Spencer Hartford?'

'Yeah. His wife. Whys that?'

'How'd she die?'

'Suicide.'

Nick heard a hand go to the handset again and muffled words. 'Hey, can I call you back in five?'

'No worries,' he replied, slightly confused.

Chapter Three

Nick made it back to the police station without the phone call from his chief that he'd been expecting. The station was a brick veneer building with a tiled roof that looked straight out of the 80s. Inside, the décor matched the exterior, and he felt like he was transported back to some of the stations he had spent time in as a rookie.

Nick placed the rifle in the clear evidence bag down on the table in the centre of the offices as a small group converged. The local sergeant and detective stood to his left, alongside two younger constables. 'Found it about a hundred metres from where the body fell,' he said.

The detective, Ned Trottman, picked the gun up and held it in his hands. 'Shit, I didn't think you'd have any chance. The current out there's flyin' at the moment.'

'Lodged under a tree root, apparently,' he replied. His phone vibrated in his pocket, and he pointed toward the interview room. 'Can I take this in there?' he asked the sergeant, who gave him a thumbs up in reply.

Nick answered his mobile on its third ring as he closed himself in the interview room and took a seat. 'That was longer than five minutes,' he answered to his boss.

'You alone?' the chief replied. He could tell by his tone it was serious.

'Yeah. Back at Collie station. What's wrong?'

'You said Spencer Hartford's wife is dead?'

'I did?'

'Listen. I'm going to email you through a couple of things when I get a chance. For your eyes only for now, alright?'

Nick was confused. 'What's this about, chief? You're acting strange.'

'I investigated the death of a young woman twenty years ago. Her name was Linda Mattazio. She was found in bushland on the outskirts of Dubbo, strangled to death. The case was unsolved, I just couldn't crack it. It's one that has gnawed at the back of my brain for a long time.'

There was silence at the end of the line. 'And?' he replied.

'And Spencer Hartford was our number one suspect.'

Nick paused in shock. He had met Spencer only once, a few months earlier, when they had been invited to dinner when the couple were in Sydney. He was a nice enough bloke, a little too smart for his liking, and he thought he used a lot of big words to show off. He knew he was a lawyer turned politician, and after listening to him speak throughout the night, he thought he may just have the brains and charisma to do a decent job in the profession.

'Liberal member Spencer Hartford? Are we thinking of the same person?' he asked.

'Yep. He was dating Linda at the time. They went to university together. Love of his life, apparently. I'm one hundred per cent sure it was him who did it. But I could never pin it on him, never got close. Everyone screamed at me that it was him, but we had nothin'. Parents were loaded back then, and he got a lawyer real quick.'

'Are you sure it wasn't the parents just trying to keep him out of trouble?'

The chief sighed. 'Look, I interviewed him twice. Once formally, and once not, and I like to think I have a pretty good gut feel on a person, you've got the same gift. Both times I spoke to him, I was convinced that he was my prime suspect.'

Nick felt his phone vibrate in his hand again, and he was sure it would've been Bec asking when he was coming home. 'So, what are you thinking?' he asked.

'I think you head down to Edithvale with Bec and be a supportive partner. I'm not saying he has anything to do with this at all. And I remember you mentioning back a while ago that Bec's best friend had some problems. It could just be exactly what they are saying.'

'And if it isn't?'

'Just keep your eyes open is all I'll say.'

Nick hung the phone up and sat in the silence trying to re-calibrate his thoughts. He'd only met Spencer Hartford once and hadn't truly got a measure of the man through the one encounter. He opened Google on his mobile, typed in his name and looked at the first news article headlines that came up.

"Spencer Hartford, rising star in state politics, has not gone unnoticed in Canberra."

"Hartford confident in vote count."

"Push from PM for Hartford's entry into inner circle."

Nick had heard from Bec about her best friend's partners rise in local politics, from a popular local solicitor to local councilman and then the meteoric rise from state to what was looking like a role in federal politics. He knew in the last election that the Liberal party had won, and his seat in the Farrer region had helped strengthen the bond the farming communities had with his political party.

Nick wished the local team good luck with the case, and promised he would try his best to be back soon to assist, but deep down felt like they may be grasping at straws. The gun was a big win for the team, but he felt with gangland style murders like this that most people who were committing them were smarter than the usual batch of criminal. He had just turned onto the busy Sturt highway when Bec rang again.

'Hey, I've just left Coleambally now. Maps says six hours until I'm home,' he said.

'Did you see my texts? I've booked a flight direct to Edithvale. Is there any chance you could meet me there?'

Nick indicated and found a spot on the busy highway to come to a stop. 'Yep. I can. It's a bit further than six hours, though. I'll try and make it there tonight, or I may stop off. I'll keep you posted.'

'No worries. Spencer is meeting me at the airport to pick me up,' she replied.

Nick tensed up at Spencer's name. 'Oh. Are you sure?'

'Of course, what's wrong? You're sounding weird.'

Nick cleared his throat; he needed to remember to reserve his judgement and keep the chief's information to himself for now; he didn't need her worrying any more than she probably was already. 'Yeah, all good. I'll let you know how I'm going.'

Nick indicated back onto the state highway, and after an hour, hit a major intersection. Left to Sydney, right to Edithvale. He hadn't been south of the state for months. And hadn't been back towards his hometown for over a year, even though he promised himself over and over that he would. He knew returning to the region he was from might bring up old wounds, and some that were still fresh. He had been part of a murder investigation in his hometown a while back, on the hunt for a killer of local women. After identifying the culprit, he was given the luxury of investigating his own mother's cold case murder, in which, to everyone's surprise, he solved and apprehended his own mother's killer. The whole ordeal had scarred him though, and made him feel like he never really wanted to go back. His sister Jess was the only thing tying him there now.

The Hume highway was long and straight as an arrow in many sections and ran from Sydney to Melbourne. Constructed in the early 20th century, it was one of the busiest major highways in Australia and a key trucking route used for interstate transport. As he waited for a clear run in the traffic to turn, he watched a group of giant road train trucks fly past in the direction of Melbourne. Once clear, he turned out behind them and sped up to a comfortable speed. He had spent considerable time in the last two years traversing the major highway, while he investigated some of the more serious homicides in the state. It wasn't how he thought his career was going to go when he thought about it, but now he couldn't imagine being a part of a bigger team anymore and enjoyed the autonomy his role brought.

Nick's phone rang again, and he looked at the name on his car screen. 'Prue Thornton.' He had a fair idea what her call would be about, and let it ring out. She was a famous reporter and podcaster and had helped assist him in a case searching for a missing woman. He assumed she may have got wind of Emily's death and was sure she wanted some more information. The young wife of a promising young politician dead. It would be a story every major news outlet would want to get a hold of.

Chapter Four

Linda stood in front of the mirror in her bedroom and eyed her outfit. Her denim miniskirt was shorter than she would usually wear, and she knew her mother wouldn't approve, but hoped she may be able to sneak out before she noticed. She was nineteen years old; her mother couldn't be the boss of her forever.

Her family was close-knit. Old school Italian. And very old-fashioned. She wondered what they would've thought about her new boyfriend, Spencer Hartford. She had met Spencer in her first year at Griffith University and, after a short courtship, had begun dating. Some of her new friends at university hadn't approved, saying that he was a lady's man and would break her heart, but they didn't know the Spencer she knew. He was kind, caring, and could make her laugh. He was the perfect man. She desperately wanted to tell her mum about him, but knew she wouldn't approve. It was her little secret to keep alone for the time being.

She'd got back home to Smith's Creek a week earlier and had spent the week working at her parents' grocery store in town. On her third day behind the counter, she finished serving a local farmer whose son she'd been to high school with.

'Good to see you again, Larry. Tell Craig I said hello.'

The farmer grabbed his grocery bags and returned her smile. 'Will do Linda, you say g'day to your mum for me as well.'

Linda waved him off and headed back down to the aisle behind the registers. Their shop was small, and as the bigger grocery chains moved into the surrounding towns and took more and more of the market share, she wondered just how her mum and dad might survive in the future. As she looked around at the wire shelving, ancient cash register, and well-worn lino floor, she knew her future wasn't here. It was in Sydney or Canberra, as a lawyer. Her first year in law had gone well, and she was top in her year alongside Spencer in nearly all of her classes, and she imagined them as a power couple, working side by side in the Supreme Court on some of Australia's biggest cases.

Linda packed the soup cans one by one on the shelf, slowly and meticulously. She knew how picky her mum was about the shelves and could hear her in her head, chastising her when she was younger for her lackadaisical approach.

'Fancy seeing you here,' came a voice from right behind her.

Linda jumped in fright and dropped two of the cans on the floor, causing red tomato soup from one of them to explode all over her and the customer's feet, which she saw first before their face. She looked up in shock and saw Spencer standing in front of her with his cheeky smile.

'You nearly scared me to death!' she said with a smile.

Spencer looked down at his feet. 'Sorry! I thought you saw me. Jesus, looks like a crime scene now.'

'I'm sorry, let me go get a mop.' She walked off toward the rear of the shop to where the cleaning supplies were, feeling slightly confused. Spencer lived an hour away, on his parent's farm, and told her he was going to be working all week and couldn't see her. They had been speaking mostly by text over the last few days, and he never mentioned he was planning to visit.

Linda came back and started the clean-up process while Spencer finished loading the shelves. As she drained the last bit of tomato soup mixed with water into the mop bucket, she stood up and eyed his handy work. 'You looking for another job?' she asked with a chuckle.

Spencer gave her a wink. 'I've got more than enough on my plate, thank you, miss. Sorry about all this,' he said, pointing at the mop and paper towel.

Linda laughed. 'Don't be. It's the most excitement I've had all week.'

Linda walked back up to the front counter to check no one was up waiting to be served. Seeing the shop empty beside her and Spencer, she leaned against the counter and handed him some chewing gum. 'You want some?'

His eyebrows rose. 'Why? Does my breath stink?'

'Don't be silly, of course not.'

Spencer grabbed a piece of the sweet-scented gum and put it in his mouth. 'So how did I not manage to ever see you around before university?'

Linda shrugged. 'Well, remember, you went to boarding school, and I went here.' She laughed. 'And I don't think your parents would ever shop here.'

Spencer's parents were old money. They had owned their property, "Hartford," for over one hundred years. Originally a cattle farm, they had begun planting grain crops at the turn of the century with resounding success. They were one of the first farmers in the state to have a successful rice crop after Spencer's great-great-grandfather was given rice seed provided by the N.S.W government on an exchange program with Japan for supplies pre-war.

Spencer frowned. 'And why would you say that?'

It was his one fault sometimes, Linda thought. He was so insulated from the struggles of the regular population, and he sometimes lacked tact. 'Because look at this place, Spence. I think your mum might head to Dubbo instead of coming here.'

Spencer looked around. 'Maybe. Well, I'm going to recommend it here. This place is nice.'

She knew he was just trying to save face. 'Thank you.'

'Now. What time do you finish? Wanna' go for a drive?'

Linda looked at her watch, which read four o'clock. 'Yeah, sounds good. Mum should be home any minute and I can pack up.'

'Sounds good. I'll go wait in the car.'

'Don't you want to meet my mum?' she asked.

'I, uh, maybe next time, yeah?'

Linda was a little disappointed, but knew that it was all pretty fresh, and maybe he didn't feel comfortable meeting her parents just yet. He seemed to be able to mould seamlessly into any conversation or environment, and was immediately likeable, and she was sure her parents would love him, but decided to not push the issue. 'Fair enough.'

After a quick change over with her mum, and an inspection of the aisle she had just finished packing, much to her frustration, she ran to the back of the store where their home was and got changed in her bedroom into shorts and a white singlet. She smelt her armpits and grimaced, and then quickly sprayed herself with her body spray and headed for the door.

As she walked past the front register, her mother spoke to her back. 'That your new boyfriend out there?'

Linda blushed. 'No. Just a friend.'

'Well, make sure you tell him we don't bite. I'd like to meet this mystery man someday.'

Linda waved her mother off. 'You will,' as she headed for the front door. 'Bye.'

As she stood back in her room in front of her mirror two weeks later, getting prepared to go out for dinner with a few of her friends for the first time since she had got back to town, she thought back to that magical afternoon and night. He had prepared a picnic for them both and they had sat by the riverbank on a rug and drank wine and eaten cheese. She had sat on that same riverbank many times in her youth, but knew as the sun went down behind the gum trees that this night was different, and she was prepared for what she hoped was going to happen next. They made love on that rug when the sun had finally set. It was her first time, which he knew, and it was a little awkward, but Spencer had taken it slow and been a complete gentleman, and now, standing back in her bedroom she felt a love that she had never felt before in her whole life. She wanted to be with him, and be with him forever.

Chapter Five

Nick had made the call three hours away in the darkness that he would press on and make it to Edithvale before stopping for the night. He pulled into a service station in Jerilderie and grabbed a can of Red Bull and a packet of snakes for a sugar hit as he put another tank of fuel into his car.

The highway between Jerilderie and Milford was dead flat and wide, with sparse paddocks stretching as far as the eye could see on each side of his car. He knew that late at night was the perfect time for kangaroos to be out and about, and he was on high alert, knowing how big they grew out here, and the damage they could do to a vehicle. He looked down at his phone to check the range, which now read zero bars of reception, and his mind wandered back to a memory of being out on another rural highway like this one as a young policeman, stuck with a damaged car.

Thankfully, he didn't see any more kangaroos on the empty highway, and wasn't surprised to see only the lonely truckers traversing the empty road. He knew the road well. Just outside of his hometown, Milford, where he grew up, he started to see familiar landmarks and the gates of the farms his father had worked on as a shearer when he was a child. Coming over the slightest of rises, Milford lay before him, with only a small smattering of lights spread over the horizon. The town was small, with a population of only three thousand, which dwindled every year, and had seemed to worsen after COVID and the heavy restrictions the state government had put on the regional towns.

Nick slowed on the town's outskirts as memories of his childhood came flooding back, and as he crossed the bridge over the river coming into the town centre, he looked out at the dark water longingly. His childhood had been spent in the waterway, and he didn't have a single unhappy memory there. It was other places in the town where his memories were not as great. He continued through the town, past the entrance of the street where his childhood home sat, and almost wanted to turn in and take a quick look before he thought better of it, and accelerated back out onto the highway, now only an hour away from Bec and Edithvale.

The last leg of the journey had been difficult, and he had cracked both of his front windows and turned his stereo up to keep himself awake to make it safely into town. As he came into Edithvale and pulled into the Paddle Steamer Motel, the digital clock on the dash read 4am. He found room thirteen easily and snuck in through the door Bec had left open, got undressed, and slipped into bed beside her.

Bec rolled over in his direction, and through the outside light on the front porch, he could see her smile. 'I thought you may have stopped,' she said.

Nick smiled. 'Nah. Sorry I didn't text. No range til' you get to Milford. Thought I'd push on through.'

Nick wrapped his arms around her and she nuzzled into him. The room was cool, and he was dead tired. He heard her say something else to him, and he didn't even have a chance to answer before his eyes were closed and he was in a deep sleep.

The next morning, he was awoken to warm sunlight cascading over his face through a sliver in the curtains. He could smell coffee and could hear the shower running. He sat up and looked around the motel room. The walls were red brick, and the interior was modern and spacious. The air conditioning worked well, and he knew Bec would've made sure of that before she booked. He was a hot sleeper and struggled without a fan or cooling on in his bedroom at night.

Nick got out of bed and padded over to the open bathroom door to a glorious sight. Through the thick mist of the boiling water, he eyed Bec in the shower as she cleaned her hair. She turned and smiled in his direction. 'Good morning, thought I'd let you sleep.' He removed his boxer shorts and jumped into the shower with her. He had to adjust the shower head as he stepped in as he was over a foot taller than his partner, so showering was sometimes an awkward proposition. He held her as the hot water ran over his shoulders and he could feel her body fold in on his as she burst into tears.

'I, I, I can't believe she's gone,' she cried.

Nick patted her back and held her. He had felt more than enough loss in his own life, and knew that sometimes words were best left unspoken. He knew, although they had lived a long way apart, that she and Emily had been extremely close, and had text and sent each other voice notes daily. Many a time he had seen her entranced on the couch, with her headphones in, listening intently to another of Emily's long-winded voice notes. He always would laugh and wonder; why didn't they just call each other? But he heard that Emily was a workaholic and assumed that maybe, with her long working hours that it was easier to communicate that way.

After they had got out of the shower and got dressed, Bec made them both another coffee from the small pod machine above the bar fridge on the bench. He sipped the bitter coffee and grimaced.

'You're such a snob,' she said with a laugh.

'You'd think after all of the terrible coffee I drink on the job that I'd have better tolerance for it.'

Bec sat on the edge of the bed in black exercise legging and a sports bra. Her long black hair was tied up in a messy bun, and although she wore no makeup, he couldn't imagine how it could make her look any better at that moment. Her skin was a dark coffee colour, and her eyes were a striking dark brown. She always laughed at him when he told her she looked like a Bollywood actress, but with her Indian heritage and her striking beauty, he was surprised she couldn't see it herself. Looking closer, he could see that she looked like she had been through the wringer over the last 24 hours, and for the first time in their relationship, he was almost lost for words. There was nothing he could say that was going to make it better.

'How was the flight?' he asked.

She sipped from her mug and wiped the last of her tears away. 'Fine. We got in half an hour earlier than expected.'

'And did Spencer pick you up?'

'Yeah. He asked if I needed a place to stay, but I told him I'd already booked this place.'

'Awfully kind of him.'

Bec's eyes narrowed suspiciously. 'What's your deal with him, anyway? You didn't seem happy with him picking me up?'

'No deal,' he replied. He wanted to keep his suspicions regarding Spencer and what the chief had told him earlier to himself for now. He could see Bec was fraught with emotion, and adding what he knew right now wouldn't have been smart.

'He's a good guy, Nick. I know it. I know men like him aren't your cup of tea. But just for me, today, please just be here for me.'

Nick walked towards her again and wrapped his arms around her. 'You know I will. I'm sorry.'

Edithvale was busy. It was a thriving town with a good problem to have, being stuck with two major incomes: farming and tourism. In the winter, the town hummed with activity, with busy farmers and families in preparation for planting their crops and people coming far and wide for one of the biggest sheep and cattle sales in the state. In summer, the town filled with southerners from Melbourne, itching to head up to the warmer climates to use the Murray River for waterskiing and fishing. He remembered as Edithvale filled up more and more each summer that the run-off of tourists were beginning to continue up further north toward Milford, his hometown. It was a great problem to have, there were just too many tourists for the region.

They stopped in at a local coffee shop that he remembered from his last trip to town and took a seat. A young waitress came up and took their order without writing it down and hurried away.

'I hate when they do that,' he said.

Bec was engrossed in her phone and looked up with a smile. 'You sound like an old man. Stop being grumpy.'

Nick sat quietly and read through emails on his phone. The detective from Coleambally had emailed him overnight to say the gun had been sent off for further testing. He knew what the result was going to be. He had another from Sergeant Ruby Zhao, from Riema, a little town on the coast where his holiday home sat, thanking him for his 'anonymous donation' toward their brand-new police station, which had just finished construction.

'Spencer's going to meet us at the house,' Bec said, snapping him from his daydreams of the beach.

Nick looked up, and soon came to the realisation that he hadn't even asked Bec where Emily had died. 'Their house?' he asked. The home was down the eastern end of town, towards the river, near the police station. It was always near the river where the first homes were constructed back in those days. It's where the wealth was generated. The heritage came after, and now it was what the locals called 'the rich end of town.'

'Yes, their house. That's where it happened.'

Nick stood awkwardly as the subject came to the forefront and looked his partner in the eyes. 'Did he, ah, say how she did it?'

Bec shook her head. 'No. Not yet.'

Nick breathed a sigh of relief, like not knowing the method of it somehow made it better for the time being. 'Fair enough.'

After a run-of-the-mill country big breakfast and some halfway decent coffee, they made their way down toward the river end of town. The river port was full of tourists, and they slowed to follow a horse-drawn carriage which had Japanese tourists sitting on the back of it, taking photos and smiling. The buildings around the port were the oldest, and it was the busiest port in the state back in the late 1800s due to the paddle steamer boats that were needed to transport supplies from town to town back then. The flagship building in the port was the Edithvale Hotel that sat on the corner. It dwarfed the shopfronts on either side of it with a sheer white colonial façade that looked to have just had a fresh coat of paint for the season. It had ornately carved wide columns; that supported a full top floor veranda. Although similar to many of the pubs he had drank at over his lifetime, it always had a special place in his heart from his memories as a kid spent in there with his father.

Heading past the pub and through the port, down towards Cadell Street, they passed the police and ambulance station and made a left turn closer to the river. Cadell street was wide and perfectly manicured, with blossoming Jacaranda trees lining the street. Bec marvelled at the sight of the beautiful trees. 'Wow.'

'Looks like we're in the fancy end of town, that's for sure.'

'Wait until you see the house,' Bec replied. 'Just here on the left.

Chapter Six

Nick slowed the car and parked across the road. The home had a white picket fence around waist high, spanning the width of the block, and on the right-hand side neat black electric gates stood open. A brick lined driveway ran on a slight angle toward the home, which in his opinion looked absolutely beautiful. The home was clearly built in the early 1900s and was of federation style. It was built with red bricks and had a giant dark green gable over the front stained-glass windows. To the left of the gable was a front porch, which spanned the width of the block that had an intricate balustrade. The gardens were immaculate and behind the white picket fence and running along the front porch were expertly trimmed hedges. Someone had taken real care here, he could see.

As they got out of the car and crossed the road, he eyed the back of the roof line. Above the terracotta tiles was a black metal clad wall, which rose above the building ominously. It looked like someone had dropped a spaceship on the back of the home.

Bec watched Nick's eyeline and commented, 'Renovations. They had just finished a big extension.'

Nick grimaced. 'Not my cup of tea.'

'I guessed as much. What about the front?'

'Much more my taste. It's a beautiful home.'

They walked down the mouth of the driveway and up the stairs to the front door. He pressed the doorbell, and they stood and waited. While they stood, he looked up at the inside of the porch and eyed a camera blinking in their direction. He wished all homeowners took their security as seriously. Good footage was invaluable for investigators.

Nick heard a lock click, and the door creaked as it opened inward. Standing in the doorway was Spencer Hartford, Emily's husband. He wore neat khaki chinos, and a white dress shirt, which he could see by the symbol was Ralph Lauren. His hair was brown, with slight wisps of grey running through it and slicked back neatly. He wore glasses and was clean shaven, and for someone whose wife had died, looked far fresher than what he was expecting.

'Nick? What are you doing here?' he asked.

Nick was taken aback, and as his mouth opened, Bec looked in his direction and spoke for him. 'He's just here for support, Spence. For me.'

Spencer blinked slowly. He watched him process his thoughts and knew how different people dealt with grief. Confusion and anger were common. He held out his hand in Spencer's direction. 'I'm sorry for your loss, mate.'

Spencer looked down at his hand and then shook it. With a sad smile, he replied, 'Thank you, please, come inside.'

Bec walked in first and gave Spencer a hug. As Nick stood awkwardly behind the couple at the threshold, he looked down the long hallway. The walls were painted dark red, and he could see photos hanging from frames lining each wall. To the left of the front door was a black-and-white image of Emily and Spencer from what looked to be like when they first met. Her smile was infectious, and he remembered back to when he met her with fondness. It was always the ones you least expect; he thought to himself.

From the end of the hallway, he watched as a small bulldog came bounding down, with its ears back and a happy grin. It ran straight past Bec and Spencer straight to him, and he knelt down to greet it.

'That's Remi,' Spencer said.

Remi was a beautiful caramel colour bulldog with big spoon ears. She looked up at him and licked him on the face. Her nose was squashed up, and she snorted happily. 'Well, hello beautiful,' he said, giving her a scratch.

Bec shrugged as they watched him. 'All dogs love him,' she said with a laugh.

Nick walked down the long hallway with his new friend by his side and stood at the end of the hallway. He looked around the room at what looked to be the new extension. The rear of the house was enormous, and ultra-modern. It had polished concrete floors, which he could feel through his socks, seemed to be heated. The kitchen was gloss white and spacious, and the bench tops had the same polished concrete as the floor. The whole back wall of the building was lined with floor-to-ceiling glass, and the lounge was sunken down two steps across from the kitchen.

'You have a beautiful home,' he said in Spencer's direction.

'Thank you,' Spencer replied, standing behind the island bench. 'You guys want anything to drink? Tea? Coffee? Something stronger?'

'I'll have tea, thanks,' Bec replied.

'Just water for me, mate,' he added.

After making Bec a tea and handing Nick's water over the bench top to him, Spencer walked over to the dining room area beside the kitchen, and took a seat. They sat down across from him, and Nick watched Spencer as he spoke furtively. The detective in him, unable to fully switch off, was unable to ever not have a small inkling of suspicion. He had all the hallmarks of a grieving widower, but what his chief had told him about the murder investigation from the past seemed to have lit something in his brain to put him in this mode. He questioned every comment, every gesture, and was keen to hear more.

Spencer continued speaking to Bec. 'I just don't know. I've been away so much. I've been so busy with work, and I haven't been home a lot. I'm sure you've heard.'

Bec nodded. 'Yeah, she said you've been in Canberra a lot only the other day.'

'Rising star, they say,' he interjected.

'So, they say. It's not all as glamorous as the papers make it out to be, sadly, mostly just people in small rooms backstabbing each other.'

Bec gave him a look that he now knew only too well, it was that look that said leave it alone. He sipped his water and let Spencer continue to speak. 'Like I said, I've been away so much, and I know she's been really busy with the last few cases she's been working on. Anyway, she had been to see a therapist a few months ago about her some of her issues and she was feeling really positive about it all. We'd been away last month up to Queensland and only just got back the other week. I had to head back to Canberra.' Spencer's voice cracked as he spoke. 'And I hadn't heard from her in a day. It was weird. She was always texting.' Spencer chuckled and glanced up at them, and he could see tears in his eyes. 'So naturally, I started to panic.'

'So, what happened? Who found her?' Bec asked.

Spencer sighed and wiped his tears away. 'We have a grocery delivery service. Manny is the guy's name. Pops in and out of our place from time to time.'

'But how did he get in?' he replied.

'He usually comes in through the side gate and comes through the back door. We leave it open for him. He had a trolley with cold packs for the meat and vegetables that can't go up the front stairs.' Spencer sipped from his coffee and looked out the windows toward the back garden. 'He found her in the back yard.'

Chapter Seven

Linda sat with her best friend, Katie, and watched as she rubbed tanning oil on her arms. The beach on the riverbank was busy with many people she knew, and a lot of tourists she didn't. The sun was high in the sky, and she could feel her fair skin burning.

'You want some of this, Linds?' Katie asked, passing over the oil.

Linda looked down at the bottle, and the SPF rating, which was zero. Her parents used to laugh at how fair she was, and her dad would often ask her if she was even Italian. Surely abit of this oil wouldn't hurt, she thought. 'Yeah, sounds good.'

Linda rubbed the clear oil over her arms, and then let Katie rub the oil across her shoulders and the back of her neck. Once Katie had finished, she sat back down on the towel on her stomach, and pulled her bathers down low, right to the top of her bottom.

'Cook me, sun,' Katie said with a laugh.

Linda looked at her friend in her red bathers. They were tiny compared to her more conservative black swimsuit. Katie had stayed behind in Smiths Creek to help look after her sick mother, who was dying of breast cancer. She felt sorry for her best friend, who had to basically sacrifice the prime years of her life, to stay behind at home to look after her while Linda headed off to university. All of the parties and stories that she had, she felt like she had to keep to herself, because she felt bad that her best friend was missing out on so much.

'How's your mum going?' she asked.

Katie sighed. 'Good days and bad days. We've got another round of chemo in Sydney next week, so hopefully we make some progress.'

'Well, you know if you need anything at all, I'm here to help.'

'Thanks.' She rolled back over onto her back and put her sunglasses on as a group of boys walked close to their towels. 'Now, tell me everything about this new man!'

Linda smiled. 'Where do I begin? His name is Spencer. His parents are farmers. Live about an hour out of town..' Katie cut in. 'Wait. Where did he go to school?'

Linda shrugged. 'Boarding school. One in Sydney.'

'Right. So, sounds like he's loaded,' Katie replied.

'Yeah, his family is well off, but it's more than that. He doesn't even talk about money with me.'

Katie laughed. 'Yeah, people with money never talk about it. They don't have to.'

Linda could see her point. 'I guess. Anyway, we met in class. He's brilliant Katie, top of our class, tall, nice hair.'

'Sounds like he's got it all.'

Linda sat back and looked up at the sky with a smile. 'And we did it.'

Katie shot up and rolled in her direction. 'Linda Mattazio! What!'

'Yep. Two nights ago.'

'Where? Surely not at your mum and dads?'

Linda grinned. 'Pretty much right where we are sitting.'

Katie stood up impulsively and screamed. 'You did not! Oh my god!'

'Well, not right here. But yeah, on this beach.'

'Wow. Well, that's abit more romantic than my first time, in the back of Brayden Morton's ute.'

'You could say that. Honestly, it was pretty perfect.'

'So, when do I get to meet Mr. Perfect?'

Linda looked out across the river and thought about it. Her romance with Spencer had been amazing, and fast, and she wondered how bringing her friends and family into the picture would change things. It was still all so fresh, and she worried about what other people would think. Spencer was an amazing guy, but she knew his wealth sometimes showed to the average person, and she didn't want her best friend, or any of her friends for that matter, having an opinion of him that she didn't like.

'Soon,' she replied.

The girls finished up at the beach as Katie continued to pepper Linda with more and more questions about Spencer. They bid each other farewell shortly after and Linda made her way home to help her mum close the shop up for the night.

***

Spencer sat at the dinner table in the dining hall of his home and listened to his mother and father talk. His grandfather sat opposite him sipping a small crystal glass of what he assumed was port or sherry. To the left of his grandfather was his little sister, Lisa, who was a year younger than him, and at this moment seemed to be the new family favourite after winning her third equestrian event for the year.

'As I was saying,' his mother continued. 'If Lisa keeps this up, we're going to need to look into expanding the parade ground. We'll need a bigger stable.'

'And another horse too, mum,' Lisa replied, with a mischievous grin in Spencer's direction.

'Yes, another horse, too. If we are going to be competing on a national level, you'll need the best.'

Spencer's father sat at the end of the table, and sipped from his bottle of beer, watching the two women speak. Spencer admired his father deeply, and the two were extremely close. Their family had grown up on the land and were one of the wealthiest families of landowners in the state. His father was an everyman. He was just as comfortable speaking with other farmers at a sheep sale as he was in a fine dining environment with his mother in the city. He could assimilate into any situation, and it was a trait that Spencer tried his best to copy.

'And who will look after all these extra horses?' his father replied.

'Grandpa can,' Lisa replied, placing her hand on her grandfather's. 'He loves the horses.'

Spencer's grandfather, John, huffed and replied, 'Sure, give the old fella another job.'

'You know you're perfectly entitled to say no one of these days, John,' his father said, as he turned his attention to him. 'So, Spencer, how has your first year of university been? You haven't told us a thing?'

Spencer sipped from his beer and chose his words carefully. His parents were very much hands off in all of his schooling, and they rarely asked for any progress, but he knew they expected perfection. Although the family had made their money predominantly in farming, some of his uncles had branched out into other professions. He knew his father was initially disappointed with his decision after high school to go to university and study to be a lawyer, but if he still had that disappointment, he now didn't show it as he listened to him discussing his first-year worth of classes.

'And how are your grades, Spencer?' his mother asked.

Spencer wiped his mouth with a hand cloth that was set out on the table. Everything in the dining room was always set out immaculately. 'Top of my class,' he replied to his mother with a smile.

'And what about your new giiiirlfriend,' Lisa said in his direction.

Spencer looked up at her with a glare that said, stop talking right now. He didn't want his parents to know about Linda just yet. He wanted to wait, bide his time, and find the right moment. This was not it.

'What? You have a girlfriend, Spencer?' his mother replied.

He nodded and tried his best to figure out how to slip out of the conversation. 'I do.'

'Well. Tell us more? What's her name? What's her family's name?'

It was those words he knew that hinged on everything. His family's name, Hartford, was synonymous with nothing but the best, high wealth, and success. They were upper class. He had never heard of Linda or her family growing up, but he was sure his mother or father would know of them. They knew everyone. And he was very sure what they would think of the union.

'Linda's her name,' he replied after a beat.

'She from around here?' his grandfather asked.

'Yeah, surprised I never met her before. Her parents own that little fruit shop and grocer over in Smith's Creek.'

Spencer heard the fork clatter, and he looked over toward his mother. 'The Mattazios?' she asked.

Spencer nodded again and sipped from his beer. This will be interesting, he thought.

'Spencer Hartford. The Mattazios are old fruit farmers, lost everything in the recession back in the 90s. They are not the type of people you need to be associating with. I will not allow it.'

Spencer's father held up a hand in his mother's direction. 'Lara, please.'

His mother's face had turned red. 'No, Mark. It is forbidden. I will not allow it. We have spent hundreds of thousands of dollars on him in schooling, and he won't be running off with some poor fruit grower's daughter and fucking it all up!'

Spencer had never heard his mother swear before. His voice shook as he spoke. 'Well, I love her, and I'm not running away anywhere. I'm going to finish my degree and become a lawyer, and you'll see, we'll be great together.'

Spencer's mother rose from the table with a face full of fury. She took one last look at him, shook her head, and stormed out in the direction of the kitchen.

There was silence in the room, and by his sister's shocked face, she knew she had made the wrong decision. Spencer's father was the first to speak. 'Just be careful, mate. Not everyone has the best intentions with us all of the time. Money can change people.'

Chapter Eight

Nick got up from the table, walked to the window, and looked out into the spacious backyard. There was a pool to the left that had high glass fencing around it. The water was a perfect bright blue, and one end of it bubbled like a spa bath. Beside the pool were rolling lawns that had wide gardens on each side that both spanned all the way down to the rear fence, and to what looked like the main feature of the yard, a giant Oak tree.

'She hung herself,' Spencer said matter-of-factly as Bec gasped. 'In the Oak tree out there that we got married under.'

Nick turned back and look at Bec, who now had tears streaming down her face. He walked back into the kitchen and grabbed a glass from the sink, filled it with water, and took it over to her. She took it graciously and took a big sip as he placed his hands delicately on her shoulders.

'Where is she now?' Bec asked.

'Edithvale Coroner took her,' Spencer replied. 'I haven't seen her yet.'

His mind raced back to a memory. An old coroner smoking at his desk, and a rude receptionist. He tried to remember the man's name. 'Paul McNaughton?' he said.

'You know him?' Spencer asked.

Nick nodded. 'Yep. Met him on another case.'

'I'm waiting for a call from the Edithvale police today. They're going to let me know when I can go in and say goodbye.'

The silence in the room was deafening. He could clearly see that Spencer was hurting, and Bec looked to be an emotional wreck. He cursed himself for his initial suspicion; it seemed pretty clear to him now that there was nothing amiss here. He hated the way his brain was wired sometimes, always looking for faults, for weakness of character.

'I need some fresh air,' Bec said to him.

'C'mon, let's go outside.'

Nick helped her up, and she stumbled, slightly woozy, on her feet. He had lost many people in his lifetime, and knew the exact stage of grief she was in. The shock phase, the it's not real phase, the I can't believe it phase.

Nick walked her over to the rear sliding door and clicked the lock to open it up. He felt the air change as the door opened, with the change in pressure from inside to out that all new houses that were well insulated had. They stepped out onto the back area onto the huge deck, where he had seen many photos from Bec of her and Emily drinking wines and discussing all of the latest gossip.

As if reading his thoughts, Bec pointed at the outdoor table. 'That's where I first told Bec about you. When I met you in Milford.'

'Love at first sight, was it?'

She smiled. 'Not exactly. But close.'

Bec sat down in one of the well-worn chairs and wrapped her arms around herself in silence. He knew that she needed some time to herself and left her be. He walked down the steps of the rear deck and over to the pool. He opened the child proof lock on the glass gate and stepped onto the sandstone tiles. He walked over and knelt down, feeling the water, which was warm. He turned around and looked up at the roof and spied the array of solar panels that looked to be heating the water. He knew lawyers earned big money, and guessed Spencer must have in his time, but now, as a state politician, he wondered how that salary could support a house of this magnitude. It must have been worth millions.

Nick stepped out of the pool area and walked out onto the grass. He pulled out his phone again and typed Linda Mattazio into Google. A grainy colour photo of the young woman was the first in the images section and he clicked into it. She kind of looked like Emily, in a way. Fair hair, blue eyes, perfect smile. Just much younger. He clicked into the article about her from a website called "Bush Horror Stories" and read it through. It was never nice reading and learning how a woman had lost her life, but he struggled to see a connection with Spencer in all of this. Yes, maybe they had been lovers, but what would warrant such violent force? And he realised in reading the article that he noticed no mention of Spencer, or even a partner at all. Had his name been redacted? It was something he had heard of before. He realised that perhaps with his career in government rising, he may have decided to try and get a digital wipe done, to get his name wiped from any and everything regarding this story. It would've been a smart move.

As he read, he walked down towards the rear of the property and toward the towering Oak tree that seemed to be the centrepiece of the garden. The base of the trunk was thick, he guessed at least a metre wide, and he imagined the tree was at least 100 years old. The leaves were a bright green and in full bloom, and the branches which supported them were thick and sturdy. He looked up high at the tree, and then back at his phone, and tried to find any articles that had some different information. They all seemed to have the same standard script from the first one, probably dragged from Wikipedia, he assumed.

Nick turned and looked back at Bec, who was still sitting in the same chair, engrossed now in her phone screen and content. He placed his phone in his pocket and began to walk back up toward the house when something deep in the back of his brain lit up. He turned back toward the Oak and looked at it again, more keenly. The trunk had no visible marks on it, and from the ground to the first branch, it was over three metres tall. He walked down around behind it and tried to find one lower, but there was nothing. The first branch was easily over two metres above his hands when he reached up high. There was a small cast iron seat near the tree, and he walked over toward to it to try to move it, to no avail. It felt like it was fixed down to the ground somehow.

Nick took a few steps back and looked upward toward the branches. Something didn't feel right. He needed to keep his thoughts to himself for now, as he knew Bec would lose it if he began questioning anything.

Bec had been watching him and walked down the grass behind him. 'You okay?'

Nick turned around and looked at his partner. Her eyes were red and puffy from crying, and she held her arms around herself. He walked over once again and wrapped his arms around her in a warm embrace. 'Yeah, I'm alright,' he replied.

But he wasn't. Everything about the tree and this spot where she died seemed off. He could feel it in his gut. Something wasn't right. And he wanted to know the truth. It was becoming clear to him now that he was looking at the scene, that Emily Hartford had been murdered.

Chapter Nine

Nick left the house on an excuse that he needed to make a few urgent calls. Bec advised him she planned to stay back with Spencer to begin preparations for Emily's family's arrival in town.

Nick walked back across the road, got into his car and ruminated for a few minutes and let the cool air inside the car lower his body temperature. Something didn't seem right. And he wasn't sure if it was the bias from the chief's earlier comments, or something deep in his brain was doing its job. He was always naturally suspicious. But was he taking it too far? He took off toward the Edithvale main street and dialled his chief again.

'What's the temperature down there?' the chief asked.

'Hot. Like always. Car says thirty-six outside.'

'Jesus, I never can get used to it when it's like that. So, what's the story?'

Nick waited at the intersection for a large tractor to drive past. Something not uncommon in farming towns. 'Something doesn't feel right, chief.'

'Give me a minute.' He heard the noise of a chair scraping, and a door closing. 'How so?'

'Emily was Bec's best friend. When Bec worked crime scene services based out of here, she met Emily when she was working as a lawyer in town. They were very close then, and have stayed in contact ever since. I'd say they've gotten even closer in the past few months. On the phone all the time.'

'Hmmm,' the chief replied. 'Must be hard for Bec.'

'Very. She's beside herself, which I'm sure you can imagine.'

'So why doesn't it feel right?'

'How she did it. She hung herself. They've got a massive old place that they'd just spent millions renovating. Big backyard, pool, the works. Down in the back of the yard is a couple of hundred-year-old Oak tree. Delivery driver found her out there, yesterday morning.'

'Shit. Horrible way to go.'

'That's just it. The tree's huge, chief. No-where to climb up, nothing anywhere near it to stand on to do it.'

'What about a ladder?'

'Well, I wanted to ask. And I could be totally wrong, but Spencer never mentioned one. And I didn't think it was the right place or time to press.'

'Understood. How did Hartford seem?'

'Devastated. Confused. All gamut's of emotions.'

'Do you believe him?'

'Yet to be determined.' He turned his car into the mouth of the street that the Edithvale police station was on. 'So, what do you think we should do?'

The line was quiet for a moment. 'We need to keep this one close to the chest. Why don't you head to Edithvale police station and see Greg Baseley, the inspector up there? You can trust him.'

'I've met him. Couple of years back,' Nick said.

'Oh, that's right. You have. How about I call ahead, and I get him to set you up a little office upstairs and I'll get the full case file for the Mattazio murder uploaded onto your account. Read through that, see if you can find anything in there. We'll use that with Greg for now. That'll be what you're working on. But in the time being, maybe ask around about your friend.'

It was a good idea. He could tell Bec he had to help out the chief on a case in town, but not who or what it was related to. That would keep her at arm's length while he tried to get to the bottom of this. He knew she would want to stick around for Spencer. Plus, funeral arrangements would need to be made soon.

'That's a good idea. Although I may need some help. It's going to be delicate. I'll need someone I can trust.'

The chief grinned. 'I've had someone in mind for a while. How about I get you a partner?'

Chapter Ten

The woman stood at the entrance to the walking track beside the bridge. She had black leggings on that surely would've been cooking her in this stifling heat and wore a black-and-white striped top that was cut far too low for the officer's imagination. Her teeth, or what was left of them, were yellow and her hair was knotted and grey. She was one of the homeless of Milford, an ever-growing problem for the small police force.

She held both arms out, guarding her friend who was crouched under the bridge on the riverbank. 'Oi' don't go near him, ya fuckin' bitch!' she screamed in the officer's direction.

Senior Constable Joanna Gray had met Colleen before, many times, and had worked a full night shift the night before, and due to one of the new constables calling in sick, had told the Sergeant, Jim Turner, that she'd stay on in the morning until he organised a replacement. She was sore from over training in the gym and more tired than usual. The year had been long, and she had started to think about her time in Milford, and wonder, was she due for a change?

Joanna had to almost laugh at the predicament. If this was any other station or town, she'd have at least another constable beside her, offering her help, and with one radio call away another truck would be sent for assistance straight away. That wasn't the case here, she knew that, and the lack of resources had started to frustrate her.

'Colleen. Step aside, please.'

Colleen took a step forward, baring what teeth she had left. 'Jo, ya' can't take him in! He's me boy!'

The young man behind Colleen was her son, Hamish. He was another of the homeless population in Milford, and although they had all tried, they hadn't been able to get through to the young man. He would be nearly finished high school by now, but she heard he had dropped out in his first year. He was tall and thin, with a pockmarked face and red scraggly hair. Joanna wanted to be lenient, but as the Sergeant had said before, one day these kids are shoplifting, the next they are into much more serious crimes. Now was the time to nip it in the bud.

'I'm sorry Colleen, it's the third time this month. If he keeps this up, he'll be in juvenile detention.'

Hamish looked up at that, and he stood up to his full height. Joanna noted the scabs and scars on his arms and shook her head. One of the other cops in the station had told her she thought he might be using already.

'Hamish, I've spoken with Neil at the hardware store. He knew your dad. If you take the tools back to him, he won't press any charges. Just do the right thing, mate?'

Joanna could see the stack of new power tools that Hamish had stolen from the local hardware store in their bright blue cases. It seemed to be a common theme in town. Shoplifting was becoming more and more prevalent. Thieves stealing, and then selling the goods for drugs.

Hamish smirked. 'Don't know what you're talking about.'

Colleen stepped forward again. 'Get away from us! Can't you see we are doin' it tough?' She pointed up the riverbank in the direction of the town. 'Who cares what we take from them? They're all fuckin' loaded. And we have we got? Nothin!'

Joanna sighed and unholstered her Taser. She had rarely used it, and knew the minute it came off her belt that most people backed off. It was more a deterrent than weapon.

Hamish saw it first. 'Whoa, wait a minute.'

But Colleen had not seemed to care, and she could tell by the size of her pupils, was clearly high as a kite. Probably on ice. The minute the Taser had come out, Joanna realised she may have made the wrong decision. Colleen's face went a dark shade of red and she screamed out as she lunged toward her. 'You're not takin' my son!'

Joanna didn't hesitate as the elderly drug user jumped at her and she pulled the trigger. The two prongs shot out and hit her centre body mass, where she'd been trained to hit. Colleen looked to almost stand at attention for a second as the prongs entered her chest, and then she froze, and pitched face first hard into the riverbank. Hamish got up from under the bridge and sprinted toward his mother. 'What'd you do! You've bloody killed her!'

Joanna calmly pulled the wire ends off the gun and clipped in a fresh load as Hamish was now only two metres away. 'If you don't come with me now, you're next. Do not test me, Hamish. I haven't slept for nearly two days. And I'm not in the mood.'

Once they had carried Colleen up the riverbank into the police car, they went back and lugged the heavy boxes of tools up and put them into the back of her divvy van. She drove Hamish over to the hardware store and she looked over at his knees, which were up near his chin in the front seat of the Ford Ranger, and he looked to be sulking.

'You're lucky I don't take you to the station and book you. You know that, right?'

Hamish nodded meekly. 'You're only young, Hamish. You have plenty of chances to turn this all around,' she said.

He stared ahead out the windscreen. 'No fuckin' point. Nothin' to do in this town. Can't get a job anywhere. Everyone knows my mum.'

Joanna turned into the empty carpark of the hardware store and drove through the wide-open door into the trade section. 'Stay here,' she said to Hamish.

A young girl was behind the counter, who looked to be around Hamish's age. 'Neil around?' she asked.

'Yeah, he's upstairs. Can you watch for customers?'

Joanna nodded. Everyone was abit more trusting in the bush. After a short wait, Neil Buchanan came ambling down the stairs and over in her direction. She had met the elderly owner of the hardware shop many times and had found him to be kind and extremely generous to local community. She wasn't sure how her plan was going to go, but thought it was worth a try.

'Thanks Kelly,' he said in the young girl's direction. 'Did you have any luck?' he asked her.

She motioned for him to follow, and she opened the rear door of the divvy van where the prisoners would sit. Inside, stacked high, were the cases of tools that Hamish had stolen.

Neil eyed them all incredulously. 'Wow, that's all of them.'

Joanna grinned. 'Yep.'

'Where'd he drop them?' he asked.

'He didn't. They were under the bridge. I think he's living under there with his mother.' She pointed to the front of the car. 'They're both inside.'

Neil walked out beside the car and eyed them sitting inside, and shook his head. 'Old Joe'd be rollin' in his grave if he saw Colleen like this.'

'How long's it been this way?' she asked.

Neil wiped his glasses with a handkerchief. 'She hurt her back in the abattoirs a few years back. Doctors prescribed painkillers. I'm sure very powerful ones. She never was the same again. It's a damn shame.'

'So, do you want an apology?' she asked.

'Yes.'

Joanna walked to the passenger side door and opened it, allowing Hamish to get out. He stood beside her with his gaze fixed directly down at the concrete.

'Anything you'd like to say to Mr. Buchanan?' she asked.

Hamish looked up at Neil. 'Yeah. I guess. I'm, ah, sorry.'

Neil looked at the young man up and down and shook his head. 'You know you're a splittin' image of your old man, don't you?'

Hamish looked back down at the concrete. 'That's what they say.'

She timed her moment perfectly. 'Neil. You were only telling me the other day you can't find workers in town?'

Neil eyed her suspiciously and knew where she was heading. It only took a split second, but a smile formed on his lips, and he gave her a curt nod. 'You got a job, Hamish?'

Hamish shook his head. 'Nah. I've applied for some. But everyone knows mum.'

'I know your mum, too. I went to school with her.'

Hamish looked up at him again. 'Oh yeah?'

'Yep. She was a wild one back in those days, too. What do you say you come here and work for me?'

The young man stood up straighter, with a shocked expression. 'Really?'

'Yep. I need someone to lug around all this timber and sweep the sheds. You reckon you can do that for me?'

'Yeah, I guess.'

'Alright, come over here and I'll get your information.' The two men walked off and Joanna turned back to the car to see Colleen watching them out of the passenger window with a sad look on her face. 'Thank you,' she said quietly.

'You shouldn't be thanking me. You should be thanking Neil,' she replied. 'You need to keep him off whatever the hell he's on. Because this is his last chance.'

***

After she dropped Colleen and Hamish back off near the bridge to their campsite, she looked at the clock in her car, and couldn't believe it was already mid-afternoon. She realised she had a missed call from her sergeant, which she guessed meant re-enforcements and the possibility of sleep, so she headed back to the station.

The Milford police station was a time capsule of the extensive bush funding that all regional communities were bolstered with in the 80s. It was red brick with a tiled roof, and well due for some reworks inside. She walked through the front reception and into the back offices to find the place empty, besides the sergeant who she could see was back in his office.

He waved her over, and she walked inside. Senior Sergeant Jim Turner sat before her, with a can of coke on his desk and what looked to be a hamburger with the lot from the local fish and chip shop. She had known him now for a few years and had started to get on his case about his weight and his general health and told him he wasn't getting any younger. He looked up at her like a child who had been caught doing the wrong thing.

'I've already eaten my Weight Watchers meal for the day,' he said. 'It was bloody tiny. I'd die if I had to eat that every day.'

Joanna shook her head and groaned. 'That's the point, Sarge. You'll put yourself in an early grave if you keep eating crap like that.' She held her hands up in his direction. 'But I'm not your mother. Do whatever you want. I can't stop you.'

He pushed the hamburger away. 'Far out. Now you've made me feel guilty.'

Joanna sat down in the chair, yawned and rubbed her eyes. 'I've been up for nearly two days. Where's Lachie?'

'Says he has COVID.'

'Hasn't he had COVID like three times already?' she said, exasperated.

'Four, I think,' the sergeant replied.

'What are you going to do?'

He sipped from his can of Coke. 'That's not your problem. I just got a call from Sydney about some extra staffing and abit more cash for our budgets.'

'Long needed.'

He nodded. 'And I got another call as well.'

'Oh yeah?'

'Yep. An old friend needs a hand. You've been asked to head up to Edithvale for the week.'

'An old friend?' she asked, confused.

'Might be a chance at that detective job you always wanted.'

Chapter Eleven

Emily sat in the conference room of the law firm that she worked at and waited for her client to arrive. She looked through the mountain of unread emails from her other cases banking up and longed for another holiday. She wondered whether she should call her friend Jen from the gym and ask if she could get her husband to watch her kids for a weekend, or maybe she could ask Bec if she could get down from Sydney. She needed a long weekend away, and she knew with how busy things seemed to be getting in Canberra that Spencer wasn't going to be able to get away any time soon.

Emily pulled her phone out and opened Instagram. She opened up his page, Spencer Hartford MP, and tapped into his latest story. He was up near Dubbo, lobbying to farmers about water rights and where best to use it. He was the perfect spokesperson. His family, being in farming for over one hundred years, led him a credibility that not many other politicians seemed to have. As she tapped through the stories, with videos of him speaking next to a canal, and then a photo of him shaking hands with a farmer and smiling, she knew that he was a natural, and seemed destined for great things.

Emily tapped on the next story, which made her pause. Standing at the canal, with her arm around his waist, was his assistant, Victoria. She had been with him since his first stint in Canberra. Tall, blonde, tanned and with a perfect smile, they looked like a happy couple from the snap. She screenshot the photo and placed her phone back down on the table, shaking with anger. Something was clearly going on there, and she had noticed that Spencer had been keeping his phone extremely close to him at all times when he was home. A sure sign he had something to hide, Jen had told her. She sometimes thought of herself as maybe a little too naïve, maybe someone who just thought the best of everyone too much, but this photo was blatant. It was something she needed to keep an eye on.

'Emily, your client is here,' said a voice from the speakerphone at the centre of the conference room table.

She looked up through the clear glass windows of the meeting room to see a young woman being ushered in her direction. She smiled and waved her inside. 'Amy, nice to finally meet you,' she said to the woman as she walked in. 'Please. Take a seat.'

Amy sat down and placed her handbag on the table. She looked a couple of years younger than her, and had looked to have lived a hard life. She wasn't even sure what she was in for, and the paperwork in front of her had little information, except for her name, Amy Davidson. Whatever she was here for it wasn't going to be simple; she assumed.

Amy extended her hand out to shake hers. 'Hi Mrs. Hartford, good to finally put a face to the name.'

Emily smiled. 'Emily is just fine, Amy. So, what can I do for you?'

Amy looked over her shoulder toward the glass. 'Can anyone hear us?'

An odd question, she thought. But she knew how paranoid some people were these days. 'Not at all. This room is soundproofed. You're in a safe place. Everything you say to me is under strict client confidentiality.'

Amy nodded. 'Okay.'

The silence in the room was filled with a tension that she knew well. Amy was scared. Scared of something, or someone. 'So,' she said again, to prompt her.

'Sorry. Okay. I need legal advice. My partner is Bo Davidson. Do you know him?'

She did. She had heard of and seen Bo Davidson in the news, and in and around the local courts. He was, from what she could tell, a small-time drug dealer in town. 'Yes. I have heard of him.'

Amy picked the edge of the table with her thumb and her finger. 'Everyone has,' she said finally. 'We have a son together.' She pulled out her iPhone and slid it across the deck to show Emily her lock screen. On it was an image of her holding a smiling toddler. 'Cute,' she replied.

'That's Ned. Our son. He's two years old.' Amy began to cry, and Emily slid a box of tissues across the table in her direction. She was clearly extremely worked up. 'Thank you. Bo is tied up with some bad people. Very bad people. Italians, from up Griffith way.'

Emily knew that there was a strong connection to drugs with the town and a small pocket of Australian born Italian mafia had operated from there in 70s and 80s. Disguised as fruit growers, they would have elaborate drug operations that seemed to keep the eastern seaboard well stocked with all of the worst drugs out there.

'Understood,' she replied. 'And he needs my help?'

'He's just found out that he's been working with an undercover police officer. Someone who is deeply entrenched up there. He's been helping him. Helping them find out the true ringleaders of the whole operation. Giving the undercover cop inside information.'

'So why does he need me?'

'Because this cop is offering him full immunity from everything he's ever done. From any involvements he has had. And he wants to know the legalities of what this guy is promising.'

She listened to Amy talk and felt that there must have been something else going on. To come to her with this story, whether true or not was a little farfetched. From what she had heard, the strength of the so-called Italian mafia had begun to wane in the 1990s, and they weren't quite the powerhouse families like the way the movies portrayed them anymore. To come to her and ask for legal advice regarding the immunity was smart thinking though, and she guessed Amy was the true brains of the relationship.

'And you can't disclose who this officer is?' she asked.

Amy shook her head. 'No. No way. Bo would kill me.'

'So, whose idea was it to come to me?'

'Mine.'

'Smart decision. Well, I don't have a lot of information, but immunity is something the police can offer up, sure.' She thought about it a little longer. 'But.'

'But what?'

'But it all depends on what exactly Bo has done. And what he would need immunity for. He can't be out killing people and get off scot-free.'

Amy laughed. 'Well, he hasn't killed anyone. Well, anyone that I know of, anyway.'

'Well, I think he's in the clear, then. If he has any paperwork regarding it that you'd like to sign off or anything, I'd be happy to help.'

It looked like a weight had been lifted off Amy's shoulders. 'Thank you so much, Emily. You've been a big help.'

After letting Amy out at the front reception. Emily stood near the front door, watching her walk off toward the main street. 'What was that all about?' Leah, the receptionist, asked.

'I'm not entirely sure,' Emily replied. She headed off toward her boss's office and knocked. 'Come in,' said the voice from inside.

The office inside was nothing like the rest of the modern office building behind her. Nigel Stratton sat in front of her, behind a giant mahogany desk which had a towering wall of leather-bound books behind him. He was a sprightly 70 years old, and he still had the quick wit and tenacity of a man much younger. Tall and thin, with a thick mane of grey hair and piercing blue eyes behind neat, black-rimmed glasses, he was still a formidable figure, and was the main reason why Emily had chosen to stay in Edithvale all of this time.

He held his arms out wide and smiled at Emily. 'Emmy, what brings you in? Take a seat.'

She returned his smile and sat down on the red leather couch which backed onto the one-sided window which overlooked the office. 'What have you got me into now?'

His mouth opened, and he tried his best to act confused. 'Me? Nothing you can't sort out, I'm sure.'

He was smarter and savvier than anyone she had ever met, even Spencer, and she knew that whatever he knew, he would only let her know if she absolutely needed to know. 'How did she get onto us?' she asked.

'Who?' he asked.

'That woman who was just in here. Amy Davidson?'

'Ah, Davidson, yes. Sorry that one didn't come across my desk. Leah said she came across us on the Google, apparently. Not everything I throw your way is a curly one,' he replied with a chuckle.

Emily sat quietly and ruminated on their conversation. Something didn't feel right. 'Ok. If you say so.'

Nigel's face had a look of concern. 'Everything okay?'

Emily sighed. 'Yeah. Nothing I can't handle.'

Chapter Twelve

The next morning, Nick pulled into the front of the Edithvale police station. Bec had got back late from the Hartford's home, after helping Spencer comfort some of Emily's family members who had come over and had fallen into bed beside him with barely a whimper. He was secretly pleased, because he didn't want to tell her how he had spent his afternoon.

The chief had uploaded the full set of case files on the Mattazio murder into his system, and he had kicked back at the small table in their room and read through most of the documentation. It was rare to see the chief's name, Mark Johnson, all through the case files, and he was surprised that he had never mentioned this unsolved case any earlier. It clearly had stuck with him.

Linda Mattazio's body was found twenty kilometres from Dubbo's city centre, deep in thick bushland. He clicked through the colour photos of the day that Mark had turned up on the scene with morbid curiosity. He felt like any shock value in crime scene imagery had left him many years ago, potentially not aided by seeing his own mother's body in crime scene photography when he was younger. Linda was found face down, with her hands tied behind her back with what looked like boot laces. Her shorts and underwear were pulled down around her ankles, and he could see that it looked like she had been thrown into a ditch. As he clicked through further to images where she had been rolled over, distinct dark bruising was clearly evident around neck, and he found it odd to see that her eyes were still both closed, despite the horrors that they must have seen.

Mark and his partner, Terry, had interviewed a council worker who had found her body. Sent out to slash the thick scrubland around the town to prevent fire dangers, it wasn't uncommon to see the local council helping the fire brigade out in the bush. After initial suspicion, due to his old criminal record, he seemed to be dispelled quickly, until their next suspect was found.

That next suspect seemed to take some time, as the case file indicated that a month had passed before their next interview. Spencer Hartford, a 19-year-old university student from near Dubbo had been brought in for questioning and it seemed, reading between the lines of the report in the way that many people in his career could, that this young man seemed to rocket into the position of their number one suspect. He found the audio file for the interview and listened in and felt things starting to fall into place for him just in the way it must have for the chief all those years ago.

'This is interviewing officer, Detective Mark Johnson, at the Dubbo Police Station, alongside Detective Constable Terry Knowles. We are here today with Spencer Hartford, aged 19, and the time is 10:01am. Spencer, state your full name for the record, please.'

Nick could almost feel the tension as he listened. Spencer would've been scared. And it sounded like he was alone.

'Spencer Mark Hartford.'

'Thanks, mate. Now Spencer, can you please tell us about your relationship with Linda Mattazio?'

'We were friends.'

'Friends? Just friends? It seems like from what we heard around town, that you two were close?'

'Yeah, I guess we were.'

Another voice came into his ears, which he assumed was Terry's. 'Would you say you were her boyfriend?'

'No. Not exactly. I don't know. We never made anything official.'

'Alright then. Where were you the night of March 1st, 2004?'

'I was home. With my younger sister, Lisa. Helping her feed her horses.'

'And where were your parents?'

'Away. They had to head to Sydney for some farming gala.' There was a pause. 'I didn't kill Linda, if that's what you think. You can ask Lisa. I was home all night.'

There was silence on the tape, and he knew Mark would be choosing his next words carefully. 'We might just do that, Spencer.'

A commotion came through the tape, and he heard the sound of a door closing and raised voices. 'Did you not think to offer my services to him? I am their family lawyer.'

'My apologies, Mr. Stratton. Nothing official is happening. Just three blokes having a chat,' Mark replied.

'Well then, what's this?' came from the recorder before the recording finished. Nick had leant back in his chair, and pictured the moment in his head. A young, rich farming kid. The family lawyer who had been around for generations.

Mark wouldn't have stood a chance. He assumed the lawyer had cut the tape, and from the remainder of the case files he couldn't find anything else relating to conversation with Spencer. It looked like the family lawyer had kept him under wraps.

Back in his car out front of the police station, he got out and walked through the glass sliding doors. The police station was impressive, and ultra-modern, and was a shining example of the latest government's initiative to bolster staffing in rural stations. He walked up to the reception and watched a young officer, who was scrolling through her phone, look up at him with a shocked look on her face.

'Quiet day?' he asked.

'It's always dead-on Sundays,' she said.

'Detective Sergeant Nick Vada, here to see Inspector Baseley?'

Her eyes opened a little wider, and her face went a dark shade of red. 'Yes. Ah. Sorry, door to your left.' She pointed toward the thick glass doors beside her.

'Thanks, I know the way.' He went to walk off and stopped and thought better of it. 'Might be a good idea to keep that in the drawer,' he said, pointing to her phone. 'You never know who could be walking through those doors.'

She nodded with an embarrassed look on her face and placed her phone in the drawer. He walked through the open area in the building towards the clear glass office of the inspector. She was right. It was quiet for a Sunday. He counted only three officers at their desks, which wasn't many for a Sunday shift. He remembered his time on the streets on the weekends being relatively busy, scraping up drunks and teenagers off footpaths and dropping them home, and resolving the latest round of domestic disputes that Saturday nights had caused.

Nick walked to entrance of the door, and Inspector Greg Baseley looked up. In his early 60s, he still commanded an impressive presence, with neatly trimmed grey hair and wire-framed glasses covering his brilliant blue eyes. He also sported a dark tan and clearly kept himself in top shape.

Greg stood up to greet him. 'Nick Vada. Long time no see, mate! Take a seat! How are you?'

'Good, Greg, good. You keepin' busy?'

Greg chuckled. 'Of course. Although I'm sure you can see the place is a ghost town today.'

'I did. Sundays are usually busy, aren't they?'

'They are. Apparently, there's some big music festival happening down in Bendigo. Half the towns down there.' His mood turned sombre. 'Terrible business with Emily Hartford. Is Bec here too? How's she doing? I remember she knew Emily quite well?'

Nick nodded and remembered that Bec, working out of Edithvale a few years back in her role in crime scene services, would know the inspector. 'She did. They were best friends.'

'Terrible business. I knew Emily myself. She did a little bit of public legal work a few years back. Helped out some of the locals who couldn't afford any legal counsel.'

Nick had heard that from her during their first meeting. It wasn't uncommon for lawyers to do some pro-bono work when they were just starting out to get more experience. 'Yeah, I remember her telling me that.' He didn't want to push too hard, but wanted to know Greg's thoughts on Spencer. 'So, what do you know of Spencer Hartford?' he asked.

Greg smiled. 'He was our mayor couple of years back. Youngest to ever do it. Look, I don't have a bad word to say about the bloke. He lobbied for some extra funding, which helped in the end to build this very station we are sitting in.

But I did feel like the mayor role was a stepping stone for bigger and brighter things. He was always destined for the top.'

'Did the chief fill you in on the case I'm looking into?' he asked.

Greg shook his head and took a sip from his coffee mug. 'He touched on it. I remember him trying to chase up some leads around here on it years ago. I was flat out today, so only got some information on the vic. Sounded terrible. Odd that he's got you chasing an old case like this up. Thought you'd have something more important to do.'

Nick breathed a sigh of relief. It seemed that the chief hadn't mentioned anything about Spencer being involved in the case. And as long as Greg didn't read too deeply into the file, he could keep a lid on everything. For now. He knew he had to be careful. It seemed that the inspector knew Spencer well. He didn't want any information getting out that he was looking into Emily's death.

'I wondered the same. But I don't question the chief's methods.'

'Smart man.'

Nick gently broached the subject he most wanted to know about. 'Hey, morbid curiosity. What officers attended the Hartford residence for the suicide?'

Greg looked at him blankly, and then he typed a couple of keys on his keyboard. 'Ahhh, Jones and Navarro. Jones is my best sergeant, and Navarro is the young girl out on the front desk.'

'Poor buggers. Not a good start to any officers' day.'

'No, it wasn't. I've chucked Navarro on the front desk for the week. She seemed abit shaken up by it all.'

Nick thought back to the young woman on her phone. She would've been on it, bored, and desperate to keep her mind busy and felt terrible. He made a mental note to speak with her again as he left. 'Right, well, I won't keep you. Got a lot of reading to do.'

'Well, after the whole Belle Smith case, I reckon they've got the right man for the job.'

'Thanks,' he replied.

'Well, I've got you set up in interview room six as an office space. Oh, and your new partner is up there already. The chief said to not tell you who it was. Make it a surprise.'

Chapter Thirteen

Nick walked out of Greg's office and headed up the stairs toward interview room six. All this cloak and dagger about his help was odd. He didn't know many officers in the region personally as he was based out of Sydney, and as he got to the door in the interview room, he was perplexed.

Nick turned the handle, and to his surprise, Senior Constable Joanna Gray sat at the white desk in front of him. She had grown her brown her out since their last meeting and it was tied back in a ponytail. She stood at exactly five feet tall, and was one of the shortest officers in the state, but he knew that her looks deceived her. She was tougher than half of the male officers he had worked with on the job and twice as hard working.

She saw him as he opened the door, and her face cracked into a huge smile. 'I should've known,' she said with a laugh.

Nick returned her smile and walked over and gave her a hug. 'Jo. It's been too long. How have you been?'

Nick and Joanna had been partnered together a few years back in his hometown to investigate a murder. Through their hard work, the culprit was apprehended, and she was promoted to a senior constable. Also, during that time, she had helped him solve the decades old cold case of the murder of his mother.

'I've been great. Keeping busy.'

'And how's the Sarge?'

'He's good. I think he wants to retire soon. I've been pushing him to clean up his diet. I think he hates me.'

Nick laughed. 'So, how'd you get here?'

'Well, ever since we worked together, I'd been telling the Sarge that I wanted to look into being a detective. I think he didn't want to lose me, and I was sure he hadn't done any work looking into it for me. We are so low on staff up there that I felt bad even asking.'

'Is it that bad?' he asked.

'It is. There's only four of us. And one of the new constables is sick every second week.'

'Shit. Sounds like it's only getting worse out there.'

'It is.'

'Well, today's your lucky day. Chief Inspector Johnson told me he had someone in mind to assist me but would keep it a surprise.' He held his arms out in her direction. 'And here you are.'

Joanna smiled as he took a seat across from her and placed his laptop and phone down on the bench. Joanna being here was a welcome surprise to him, and a smart call by his boss. He knew her to be smart and patient. Two of the main characteristics of a good detective.

'So, where do I begin?' he said.

Joanna had a thick leather-bound note pad in front of her and opened it up on the desk. 'From the beginning would help,' she said with pen in hand.

'Okay. I'm going to go back a bit. Remember Bec Ranijan from Edithvale crime scene services? We met her at the football oval back at Milford?'

'Yeah, she had the hots for you.'

'Yeah, you were right there. We've been together going on nearly a year and a half now.'

Joanna grinned. 'I knew I had a good feeling about that.'

'Anyway, her best friend is a local lawyer named Emily Hartford. Heard of her?'

'Yes. In passing.'

'Well, she was Bec's best friend. She committed suicide two nights ago.'

Joanna shook her head. 'Terrible. What a waste.'

'It is. Okay, that's the first part of the story.' He watched as Joanna scribbled notes quickly. 'Second part is a twenty-year-old case.' He opened the Mattazio case file and spun the laptop around to face her. Joanna read the top blurb out loud. 'Linda Mattazio, aged 19, found strangled to death in bushland outside of Dubbo. Unsolved after nearly twenty years.' He watched her eyes as she read down the screen and was sure of the reaction he was going to get when she saw it.

'Suspect interviewed. Spencer Hartford. As in the politician?'

'Yep.'

Joanna looked up at him as it dawned on her. 'Spencer Hartford. Was he married to Emily Hartford?' she asked.

Nick nodded. 'He was. And I believe he was involved in his wife's death.'

The silence in the room was deafening, and Joanna had a look of shock on her face. 'How?'

'She hung herself. Supposedly. A delivery driver found her in the morning, hanging from her Oak tree in the backyard. Terrified, he called the police. Police had to get the fire brigade to assist in cutting her down.' That information he had learnt from Bec through text last night. He held his phone out to her with an image of the Oak tree. 'What do you see?'

Joanna studied the phone cautiously. 'It's huge. She pointed to the branch where he was sure the rope was slung. Is that where she ran the rope?'

Nick said again, 'Supposedly.'

'Well, how did she manage to get up there? Without a ladder, it would be nearly impossible? What did the officers who came to the scene do when they found her?'

'One is quite green, and the other was a sergeant, not sure what his story is. But if I came across that, I would have been ringing alarms bells. Now, we need to tread incredibly lightly here. I want to look into this suicide and try and feel around and see if that's really what has happened here. The chief is on our side. He worked on the Mattazio murder all those years ago. So, we are going to use that as the case we are supposedly working on for now. But we cannot, I repeat, cannot, trust anybody. This is as top secret and as high stakes as it gets. If Spencer Hartford finds out we are sniffing around about Emily, who knows what will happen? I believe he has had this Mattazio murder buried. Otherwise, how hasn't any media outlets got a hold of it?'

Joanna looked at the image of the Oak tree again. 'Plus. Who knows? You could be wrong. This could be all one big misunderstanding.'

Nick agreed with her and knew it was a possibility. But he needed to go down all avenues before his mind could be at ease. 'I know it's a lot to put on your plate this early. But I want you to head up to Dubbo and speak with Linda's parents. Find out as much as you can. See if she still has any friends living around that would be willing to speak to you. If Hartford is guilty, someone might know something that wasn't spoken about back then. I'm going to sniff around town here and find out a little bit more about Emily's last few weeks.'

If Joanna was disappointed that they weren't working directly together, she didn't show it. 'Okay.' She looked at her watch. 'I'll head off now. Should make it by nightfall.'

Nick was impressed. She was clearly keen to get started. 'I'll get a room booked for you on your way up if I can find one anywhere. But from memory, Smith's Creek is tiny, so you may need to continue on through to Dubbo. Remember. Top secret alright?'

Once Joanna had packed up and left the station, he sat back up in the interview room doing some more research. He found the law firm that Emily was working for online easily, Stratton & Hartford law. He looked at the image on the top of the webpage of the partners and found the smiling face of Spencer looking back at him, along with an elderly man wearing glasses. He hadn't heard how Emily and Spencer had met, but after seeing the website, he took an educated guess. As he read through the information on the firm, something nagged at the back of his brain. He leaned back in his chair and rubbed his face, staring blankly at the back wall. Nigel Stratton, where had he heard that name before? Just as he went to click through to the next page, it hit him like lightning. He opened up the file for the Mattazio case that Joanna had been reading, and sure enough, the Hartford family lawyer's name was written, plain as day: Nigel

Stratton. So, it seemed like their ties may run even deeper than just work colleagues. He needed to ensure he kept a wide berth from Nigel Stratton. If he got any inkling that he was looking into anything, he could be trouble.

Nick finished up what he was doing and heading down past the front reception desk. He saw the young constable behind the desk almost sit up a little straighter at the sight of him, and he waited for another officer walking past to continue out of earshot before he stopped. 'Hey, constable. What's your name?'

She looked at him and replied, 'Sarah Navarro.'

'I wanted to apologise for before. I was out of line. I heard you've had a rough week.' He pointed down at her phone on the bench. 'If you need that to take your mind off things, do it, do anything you need.'

She looked at him with an appreciative smile. 'Thank you. I've never seen a dead body before.'

'It's not pleasant.'

'Hey, can I ask you a question?'

'Of course,' he replied.

'How do you handle it? How do you handle all the things you see? How do you forget?'

Nick looked at her and wondered himself. He had for a long time tried to mask his pain with alcohol, but was now going on four months sober, and he hoped to keep it that way. The bad thoughts and memories of all the murders, the loss, and the grief, was something that he struggled with every day. He thought for a few seconds as he tried to come up with an answer that would comfort the young constable. 'I'd like to give you a good answer, but I can't. Every day is different. I compartmentalise things. I push them down. Some days I talk about them, some days I don't. It all depends on how I'm feeling and what I need.'

'That's honestly better advice than I've got from most people. Thank you.'

Nick desperately wanted to ask her more about her attending the scene and finding Emily, but thought better of it. He could see she was hurting and didn't want the inspector to know he was asking around just yet. He thought leaving his phone number wouldn't hurt. 'Here.' He handed his card over the reception desk. 'If you ever need someone to talk to. Call me.'

She grabbed the card off the desk and read it. 'Thank you. I appreciate that.'

Nick headed out of the station into the bright sunshine and jumped back into his car. His options were limited, but he did know that the local coroner would gain no advantage in telling anyone that he had popped in to visit. As a detective sergeant, things were fairly open in regard to what he could investigate. Usually, he wasn't questioned.

Chapter Fourteen

The Smith's Creek local show got bigger and bigger every year, and Linda and Spencer walked through the main entrance to the football oval hand in hand. It was Spencer's first-time meeting her best friend Katie and her other friends, and if he was nervous, he didn't show it. Linda watched him as he walked and noted that he didn't seem to have his usual cheery demeanour, and wondered whether it was just nerves before the big meet and greet.

The oval was full to the brim with rides, and the sun was beginning to set over the horizon, casting the entire view in front of them in a pale purple and orange light. The flashing lights of the rides soon took over as the sky darkened, and they made their way toward their pre-determined meeting spot, the hurricane ride.

Linda prepared Spencer for the meeting. She wanted her friends to like him, so she tried her best to give him the run down. 'So, Katie and I have been best friends since primary school. She's the one that'll ask the tough questions.'

Spencer looked up at the rides and looked lost in thought. 'Hmm.'

'Are you ok?' she asked.

He looked back down at her. 'What? Yeah. Sorry. Katie, best friend, got it.'

She could feel his apprehension. 'Spence, we don't need to do this if you're not comfortable?'

Spencer cracked his wide million-dollar smile and grabbed her hands. 'Linda. Do not worry. I'm here, aren't I?'

'Linda! Over here!' came Katie's voice from near the next ride.

Linda looked at Spencer one last time, and then dragged him along behind her. Katie stood at the front of the Cha-Cha ride in a short denim mini skirt and red boob tube, which didn't leave much to the imagination. Linda imagined Spencer's judgement. It would've been much too flashy for him.

Katie held her hand out in Spencer's direction for a handshake and she looked shocked when he grabbed it and kissed it. 'You must be Katie? Linda told me all about you. Love the outfit.'

Linda smiled at Katie's shocked expression as she shouted with glee. 'You didn't tell me he was this charming!'

The trio headed along the row of rides through the throng of people towards the biggest ride in the show, the hurricane. Linda watched the ride, which had a bright yellow central pole with arms coming off in all directions like a spider. The small blue carriages flew through the air up and down, and the loud noise of a whip crack would go off whenever the carts met their highest point, as the riders screamed with a mixture of fear and joy.

Linda's other two friends, Wes and Lacy, stood near the ticket line, and Linda quickly introduced them both. Wes had been in her year at school, and they had previously dated in high school. His dad owned land, and he had followed family tradition and started working on the farm after they had all finished school. Lacy had been lucky and got out of town, and was going to university in Sydney now. She, too, was back for the holidays.

Katie interlocked her arm around Spencers and looked at the group. 'Who's coming on the hurricane with us?' she asked.

Spencer shook his head. 'No way. I don't do rides.'

'C'mon, don't be a girl,' Katie said with a laugh.

The challenge was set, and Spencer rose to the occasion. He walked up to the ticket booth and graciously shouted the group all a ride. When it was their turn to hop in the carriages, Lacy hopped into the rear one, Spencer and Katie took the middle, and Wes and Linda took the front carriage.

Once they were clipped in by the ride operator, he walked back to the ticket booth seat and grabbed the microphone. 'Okay okay okay, ladies and gentlemen, let's get this show on the road,' he announced to the crowd, who were all watching. Dance music began to blare through the speakers and then, slowly, the ride began to circulate.

'You been on this before?' Spencer asked Katie.

Katie nodded. 'Yeah, a heap of times. Bloody love it.' She looked down at Spencer's hands, which were tightly gripping the handlebar in front of them. 'You?'

Spencer shook his head. 'Nah.'

Katie took her hands off the bar and held them in the air. 'You'll be fine!'

The carriage began to rise slowly as the ride sped up, and Spencer could see the whole show from their view up high. He could see the car park and the road beyond, and he tried not to look down. He was never good with heights, but didn't want Katie to see him show any weakness. He felt the ride speeding up now, and the carriage began its descent back down to earth. He looked up ahead at Linda in the carriage in front and as the ride now hit full speed; he watched as Wes, the guy he had just met, placed his arm around her.

'How do you guys know Wes?' Spencer yelled out in Katie's direction.

Katie screamed as the ride let out a massive whip crack noise as the carriages met their full height again, and the view of the whole show was back on display. He watched as her eyes looked ahead to the carriage in front. 'Don't worry about Wes. He's harmless. He and Linda used to date when they were younger.'

Spencer looked ahead again and tried to watch their conversation. His fear of the ride and the heights was completely extinguished, as he felt a burning hot rage rising inside him. He had argued with his parents to the point where his mother was now not talking to him about this girl. And here she was arm in arm with an ex right in front of him? Why was he here? What an absolute waste of time, he thought to himself.

The ride began to slow, and Katie rested her hand on his. 'You ok, you look pale?'

He instinctively pulled his hand away. 'Yeah. Fine.'

As the carriage came to a halt, the ride operator came to their carriage first and pulled the bar up over their heads. Spencer jumped straight out of the carriage and walked down the steps without even looking at Katie. Linda watched this whole interaction as she was being let out and looked at Katie with visible confusion. 'What happened?' she asked.

Katie shrugged her shoulders. 'Beats me.'

Linda watched as Spencer stormed away in the crowd in the direction of the dodgem cars. She took chase, and soon caught up to him near the hot dog stand. She could tell he was angry, and she thought of their ride, and of Wes, and immediately realised the issue before he even opened his mouth.

'Spence, Wes is harmless..'

Spencer turned to face her and yelled. 'Do you have any idea what I've sacrificed to be here?! My own mother won't even talk to me!'

Linda looked at him with her mouth agape. 'What? What do you mean? Spence, I'm sorry.'

'Sorry?! You're sorry?!' He turned and began to walk away. 'Why don't you just fuck off with Wes if you're so keen on him.'

Linda was hurt. She wanted the night to be a celebration. And it was clear that he was taking her lifelong friendship with Wes completely the wrong way. She had never seen this side of him before. The jealousy. The anger. She secretly liked it. It made her feel an even bigger wave of affection for him. She knew he truly cared. She caught up to him and grabbed both of his hands and kissed him full on the mouth while the surrounding crowd continued on around them. Time slowed, and she felt like they were the only two people in the world. The neon lights of the show rides shone above them and the mixture of the music from all of the rides drowned out everything else. After what felt like minutes but was only seconds, she pulled back, looked him in the eyes, and smiled. 'There is no-one else, Spence. Only you. I love you.'

He stood still for a moment, and she felt all of the tension and anger slowly deflate from his body as his shoulders dropped. He looked down and she could see that he felt a little sheepish. 'I'm sorry,' he said.

'It's okay.'

'No. It's not. I just care about you so much.' He looked up at her again, and she could see the beginning of tears in his eyes. 'I never want to lose you.'

Linda never thought she would ever see this side of him. She knew he cared, but they were young, and she wasn't shy about the fact that she had seen him flirt with women back at school many times. He was a much more complicated individual than she ever thought, and seeing his emotion and the way he cared about her made her love him even more. 'You won't lose me,' she replied. 'C'mon, let's go grab something to eat and get out of here, yeah?'

Chapter Fifteen

Nick drove past the Edithvale hospital and, as he looked at the old brick building, his mind was transported back to memories of his father. The last time he had been at the hospital was to drop him off for a checkup at the cancer clinic. He had sadly lost his battle with lung cancer only a few weeks later, and being in Edithvale, so close to his hometown, meant that his family was never too far from the front of his mind. Just as he made a turn toward the back block where the morgue was located, he spied a delivery truck, which had 'Manny's fresh produce,' on the side, and slowed his car and parked behind it.

Nick got out of his car and began to walk towards the truck as the driver's side door opened. A short, thin man stepped out wearing a neat uniform and holding a clipboard and headed in his direction. He made an educated guess that this could be Manny who had found Emily's body. He chuckled at the odds. Today may be his lucky day, he thought.

Nick walked up to the man. 'Manny?'

The driver's eyes narrowed as he assessed Nick. 'Yes?'

Nick held his hand out. 'Detective Sergeant Nick Vada. You got a minute to chat?'

They sat together on the small brick wall beside Manny's truck next to the hospital and as Manny ate a sandwich; he recalled the moment he found Emily's body.

'I'm usually there earlier in the day, but my truck needed to be serviced, and I had to pick it up from the dealership. I got there about 9 in the morning.'

'What did you see?'

If Manny was shaken about it, he didn't seem to show it. Nick gauged he was in his late 50s but knew it was harder to tell with Asian men. He seemed to be of Thai or Filipino descent, and as he spoke, seemed quite stoic about the whole situation. 'I came through the back gate with my trolley and walked around the path. Headed up to the back door and went inside. I noticed wine had been spilt on the floor in the kitchen and not cleaned up, which I thought was odd, but I filled the fridge and cupboard with their order and then quickly cleaned it up for Emily.'

'That was kind of you.'

Manny shrugged. 'Emily was a good person. Very kind to me.'

'What about Spencer?' he asked.

Manny scoffed. 'Never spoke to me. Would ignore me when I was there.'

'So, what happened next?'

'I came out the back door and realised their little dog Remi wasn't inside. That's when I heard the howl. I'll never forget it. I walked out onto the back deck and that's when I saw her.' He stopped for a moment and drank from his thermos. 'She was hanging in the back Oak tree.'

'Did you try to cut her down?' he asked.

Manny shook his head. 'No. I called the police straight away. From where I am from, you do not touch the dead. Ever.'

'Last question, and then I'll leave you alone. How did she get up there? Was a ladder or a chair under her?'

Manny looked at him. 'No. Nothing. I assumed she must have climbed up somehow? I could think of easier ways to do it, though.'

He thanked Manny for his time and felt vindicated. If there was nothing underneath her, he was fairly certain she wouldn't have been able to climb up and do it the way that everyone assumed. Something wasn't right, and he jumped back into his car and drove over into the carpark behind the hospital at the entrance of the morgue. He knew if Paul would let him look at her body, it may help validate his theories.

Before he went in, he opened the favourites section in the contacts on his phone and dialled his little sister, Jess. He felt guilty that he hadn't stopped in on his way through his hometown, but planned on taking Bec out to see her and his baby nephew at Warranilla, the farm she lived on with her husband Pete.

The phone answered after one ring, and he could hear the sound of a blender in the background. 'Hello, Jess Waterford speaking.'

Forever sarcastic, he thought. 'Ha ha. Very funny.'

'Am I? Why have I heard that you are only an hour from me, and you haven't popped in yet?'

Nick groaned internally, and realised that Jack Thomson, his father's best friend, was still a police officer, and would've heard from Joanna or the sergeant in Milford that he was in the area by now. The news always travelled fast in country towns, and small things would spread like wildfire. 'I'm sorry. I should've called. It was an emergency.'

'I heard,' she replied. He heard her yell from behind the phone. 'Tim! Lunch!'

Nick loved the fact that she had named her son after his late father, and hearing his name made him happy. 'How is my little nephew going?' he asked, feeling guilty once again that he hadn't stopped in.

'He's great. Walking now. Running actually. I've been baby proofing every edge in the house. Don't worry, he's managed to find most of them, though. I swear he has two left feet.'

'Well, he's definitely yours then,' he replied with a chuckle.

'Heard about Bec's best friend. Is Bec ok?'

'Yeah. I think so. She's taken it hard.'

'What happened? I heard suicide? Did she have depression or something?'

'Something like that. Details are scarce at the moment. No note. Nothing.'

'Terrible. Just terrible.'

'It is. Anyway, just thought I'd check in quick. What do you say me and Bec come out to the farm on our way home?'

'We would love that. I bought Pete a new meat smoker for Father's Day, so he's been out in the yard every Friday night for hours, drinking and cooking meat. He'd love some new guests. I've had enough brisket and pulled pork to last a lifetime.'

Nick thought of the beautiful outdoor area on the farm nestled under the shade of the enormous gumtrees which surrounded the homestead. He heard a bang and then clatter through the line. 'Pete! Can you give us a hand in here, please! Hey bro, I've got to go, chat soon. Be safe, please.'

'Bye.'

Nick looked up at the doors of the morgue and watched as an elderly couple walked out of the building. The elderly man had his arm around the woman, and he made an educated guess that he was looking at Emily's parents as the mother looked exactly like her, only twenty years older. He stepped out of his car and walked tentatively towards them.

'Mr. and Mrs. Foley?' he said to the couple.

Emily's father looked at him, and he saw a flicker of recognition in his eyes. 'Hi, Nick, is it?' he asked.

After pleasantries were exchanged, he wished them both all the best and told them he hoped to catch up with them again soon. To see a family like this, deep in grief sometimes hit a little too close to home for him, it was the worst part of his job seeing people at their lowest ebb. He walked on past them and through the double glass doors, and spied the same receptionist as his last visit, sitting at her desk, busily typing away. Her shock of green hair from the last time he saw her had been replaced by a more subdued purple, and her colourful tattoos were covered up today by a long sleeve blouse. As he walked up to the counter, she looked up at him and did a double take; it was clear to him that this time she recognised him.

'Morning, Detective Sergeant Nick Vada, hoping to speak with the coroner if he has a spare minute?'

Her cheeks flushed red, and her face lit up in his direction. 'Nick Vada. Wow, here in my office. I heard everything about you on the Into The Flames podcast. Amazing work.'

Nick always felt odd when being complimented and said awkwardly, 'Thank you.'

'No worries at all. You're famous around here. I hear the police officers in here talking about you all the time.'

Nick believed it. His work in his last few cases had been prominent in the media, and his wasted time spent with the number of interviews he had to complete had been irritating to no end. He always mentioned how collaborative a murder investigation was, with many mentions of the large teams behind him, but that didn't seem to be romantic enough for the Australian media. They preferred a lone detective roaming the Aussie bush, solving murders at a rapid pace. It was better for the story.

The receptionist pointed him on and as he walked through the next door; he felt the temperature drop considerably as he neared the freezer section of the morgue. His memory of that receptionist on his last visit was a stark contrast to the bubbly exterior she had just put on. She barely said two words to me last time, he thought. Show's what a little bit of fame does to people. He knew he had to try and use it to his advantage from time to time.

Entering the morgue, he smelt the unmistakable smell of cigarette smoke wafting into his nostrils and was greeted by the jovial coroner at his entrance. 'Detective Nick Vada! What brings a celebrity to my little workshop today?'

The coroner, Paul McNaughton, stood at a standing desk against the side wall. He still had the same, black-rimmed glasses as Nick's last visit, and his white shock of hair still stuck up more than ever. He once again envisioned Albert Einstein as he shook his hand. 'Hi Paul. Nothing formal today. Family business, sadly.'

Paul looked confused. 'Family business?'

'Well. Sort of. Emily Hartford.'

Paul inhaled his cigarette, and he watched as the smoke slowly came out of his nose. 'Terrible. Just terrible. I saw her around the traps at court from time to time. Lovely girl. Very bright. How'd you know?'

'My partner was her best friend.'

'Well. Send my condolences. Suicide is a terrible thing.'

'It is. Hey listen, I was hoping for a favour? My partner said she couldn't stomach coming in today, just couldn't face it. But she wanted me to come in and pay last respects to her before the funeral. Do you mind if I see her?'

'Of course.' Paul turned and walked to the wall that had stainless steel doors on it, which held shelving where the bodies were stored. Nick followed and watched as he unlatched the central door at waist height. He looked over at him one more time. 'You ready?'

Nick nodded as he slid the drawer out. There was a white sheet laying over Emily's body and Paul gently grabbed each side of it and pulled it down to her waistline. He looked at her body, which, under the fluorescent lights, was deathly white. Her neck was black and blue from where the noose had sat, and he could clearly see where he thought her neck had broken.

Seeing Bec's best friend like this was not overly upsetting to him. He had seen more bodies than he could even remember, and looking down at her once beautiful face, he had a thousand questions, but knew he had to tread delicately. 'Did you do a tox screen?' he asked.

'I did. Results came back this morning. Blood alcohol level came back nearly three times over.' That was unexpected, he thought. And made him even more suspicious. 'And she also had Valium and a high level of Oxycodone in her system. Drugged to the eyeballs.'

Nick couldn't help himself. 'That's odd, isn't it? Why would she hang herself then?'

'People do odd things before death, detective. You, of all people, should know that.'

If he was shocked, he didn't show it. Just as Paul began to bring the sheet up over her face, he looked down at her arms and told him to stop. 'Stop.' Her arms were covered in deep scratch marks on both sides. 'What are the scratches from?' he asked.

'Didn't look into it. I assumed scratch marks from the branches?'

If the high blood and alcohol level was suspicious, the scratch marks all over her hands and arms, which looked awfully a lot like defensive wounds, were the death knock. Something was amiss here; it was plain to see.

'Do you want a minute?' Paul asked.

Nick shook his head. 'Sorry. No. You know how it is. Sometimes your work brain kicks into overdrive.'

Paul nodded and began to walk back to his desk. 'Oh, don't I know. Sometimes I can't separate real life from this. It's a battle.'

Nick looked at Paul as he walked away. 'Aren't you going to put her back?'

Paul lit another cigarette from his top pocket. 'Nah. Spencer Hartford is a couple of minutes away. I'll leave her out so he can say his goodbyes.'

Nick tensed up. If Spencer saw him here, he would know something was up. And worse, he might tell Bec. He had to get out of there. And fast. 'No worries. Hey Paul, would you mind keeping this just between us? I don't want Spencer knowing I got here first. Might seem a little bit disrespectful.'

'I totally understand.' Paul said with a wink. 'Your secrets safe with me.'

Nick hustled out the morgue doors and past the receptionist who gave him the flirtiest smile he had seen in a long time, and thought he was home free, until as he turned to go through the double doors, he almost walked face-first into Spencer who looked at him with confusion. 'Hey Nick. What are you doing here?'

His mind ran, and he tried his best to formulate an adequate lie. 'Just here to say g'day. Paul's an old friend.'

If his lie hadn't worked, Spencer didn't show it. 'Fair enough.'

'Where's Bec?'

'She's back at the house with Em's mum and dad.'

'Okay. I'll head over shortly.' He made his turn to leave when Spencer stepped back and put his hand on his shoulder. 'Hey, can I ask you something?'

Nick looked at him and tried to read his face. 'Yeah?'

Spencer looked over his shoulder, like he was looking for people eavesdropping. 'I wanted to ask for your help.'

This was interesting, he thought. 'Yeah? For what?'

'Em's last few days. I know she was super stressed with work. I've asked Nigel Stratton what she was working on, but he's giving me the run around I reckon. He says nothing out of the ordinary, which I don't believe. Something had to make her feel this way. I don't like it; something doesn't feel right. She was fine before I left for Canberra. I want to know why she did this. Bec's a wreck. I don't want to put this burden on her. Can you help me?'

Nick thought for a short moment and wondered whether it was a trick. It seemed genuine enough. A grieving husband wanting to know why his partner did what she did. It would give him more access to his investigation, so he thought, why not?

'Yeah, I can do that,' he replied. 'I'll do my best. But I can't promise you anything.'

Visible relief was etched across Spencer's face. 'Thanks Nick. I appreciate it. Now. I guess I better go say goodbye.'

'Good luck,' he replied.

Spencer walked off through the double doors and left him standing in the sunshine, even more confused. If he killed Emily, he wasn't acting the way a guilty man would. Why would he want him to look into why she did it? What would his motive be?'

Chapter Sixteen

Joanna had made the drive to Smith's Creek in record time. Nick had been in touch with her and helped her map out her story for anyone she ran into. They didn't need Spencer catching wind of what they were up to, and she was intrigued by the mystery of it all. Just who was Spencer Hartford? Was he a killer who had got away with murder? Or was he misunderstood? It was the most exciting her job had ever been, and she couldn't wait to get into the work.

Smith's Creek, Linda's hometown, was on the outskirts of Dubbo and only had a population of 1000. As she came past the sign for the town, she looked out into the dense bushland and noted it was a lot greener here, being a couple of hundred kilometres higher in the state than Milford. Although greener, Smith's Creek felt the same way that Milford did. A town once thriving, now left with the remnants of the old families that had been here for hundreds of years. All of their offspring were long gone, to Dubbo, Sydney and further. With all of these people leaving, she looked at what shops still remained open in the main street. Every second shop front seemed to be boarded up and as she pulled up to her destination, the Smiths Creek Hotel, she wondered whether this trip was a waste of her time. It looked like anyone here twenty years ago would be long gone by now.

The old pub was single storey and looked to be built in the late 70s with dark brown bricks. The windows were also dark brown and the only colour on the building was faded advertisements for the latest drink offerings from the bottle shop. She knew from Google that there were rooms out the back, and although she had got a full sleep the night before after her extended shifts in Milford, she yawned and stretched as she got out of the car in the fading sunlight, longing for another good night's sleep.

She never thought 24 hours ago she'd be here, working with Nick Vada again. The detective was an enigma to her. Quiet, humble and easy to get along with, she wondered how he always managed to find himself in the situations that he did. However crazy it seemed, he seemed to have a gift for solving some of the toughest cases. She hoped that he and the chief inspector would see something in her, and potentially give her a chance at trying out for a detective position with their elite unit.

Joanna walked into the pub and watched as the two older men on the bar stools turned to check her out. She wore black exercise leggings she had put on for the long drive and a white singlet top. After years in country towns, she knew that men leering was part and parcel with being a young woman in the bush. She didn't take bullshit from anyone, though, and if any of them thought to try anything, she knew she could put them on their backs in an instant.

The eldest of the two men wolf whistled at her as she walked up to the bar. 'How are ya' darlin'? Looking for a bit of fun?'

Joanna looked down the length of the bar for someone serving, to no avail. The place was a ghost town, except for the two old men. 'I'll be right, thanks. Is there someone working here or are you two just drinking for free?'

The second man looked at her. 'The owners just out changing the keg. Don't take no offence to my friend Owen here. He's harmless.'

'Yeah. That's what they all say,' she replied.

A tall middle-aged man with a round beer belly came walking out through the saloon doors behind the bar. 'Shit, sorry, had to change the kegs. You after a drink?'

She shook her head. 'No, thank you. I think someone called ahead? I was looking for a room for the night?'

'I know where she can stay,' muttered the first man under his breath.

'Drop it, Owen,' replied the publican. 'Of course, had a call a couple of hours ago.' He passed an old key on a plastic keychain over the bar to her. 'Rooms are behind the pub. You're in room six.'

She grabbed the key. 'Thanks a lot.' She held her hand over the table to introduce herself. She knew she had to get in close with the locals. It's what Nick would've done. 'I'm Joanna.'

The barman shook her hand. 'I'm Wes. Anything you need, just give me a shout.'

Joanna jumped back into her car and made her way around the back of the pub. The rooms out the back were old, and in a bad state of disrepair, but she'd stayed in worse. The air conditioner worked, the bed sheets seemed clean, and there was hot water. She had all the creature comforts she needed.

Once she placed her bags down and got settled in, she placed her timer on her phone for thirty minutes and began her yoga and stretching routine that she would complete every night before bed. She stretched out her calves, groin, hamstrings, then her lower back, until she finished with her neck and shoulders. It was rigorous, but it always helped her sleep, as she felt the release of the tension in her body after she had finished the stretches.

She woke the next morning, after a great night's sleep, and got dressed quickly and went out into the dreary morning in search of drinkable coffee. The sky was grey and overcast, and she could feel the heat coming off the road from the night before still steaming, and felt that it was going to be muggy. She set off on foot in the direction of the shops, knowing that she could see the end of the main street from the pub carpark; there was no chance she'd get lost. She guessed there were only 10-15 shops in total that still remained open as she walked past the open newsagent.

The next shop, which was a clothing store, looked to be closed down, and she eyed the cobweb strewn mannequins in the front window. It was the way of the world these days. The once thriving towns in the bush shuttering down, due to a multitude of issues that no-one seemed to be able to solve.

Two shops down was a small bookstore, which had a sign in the front that said coffee and cake and looked to be the central hub in town with the most cars parked out front. It'd have to do, she thought to herself. She pushed through the front door, and was surprised to see it relatively busy for this early in the morning. An elderly couple sat near the front window enjoying tea and cake. A younger man sat hunched at his laptop beside them, and a mother tried her best to manage a toddler who was trying to remove books off the shelves, whilst cradling a baby that looked to be only a few months old.

She walked to the counter and waited while a young girl frothed milk on the machine. She poured it into a takeaway cup and slid it over the counter at the other end. 'Matt! Latte with one.' She turned back to Joanna and smiled. 'Morning, what can I get you?'

'Just a latte, thanks.'

'Coming right up.' The girl turned back and busied herself on the machine. 'What brings you to Smith's Creek?'

'Work. I'm a journalist.'

The barista chuckled. 'And what's a journalist doing in Smith's Creek? It's gotta' be the quietest town in Australia?'

She thought there was no time like the present and went for it. 'I was on the lookout for old members of the Mattazio family.'

The barista poured the frothed milk into a takeaway cup and placed the lid on it. 'Oh yeah? Marie Mattazio owns the local supermarket. Last shop at the end of the street.'

Bingo, she thought. She had read in her case file that the Mattazios had owned the local grocery store back then. But a google search, a business search, and a phone number search had come up with nothing. She assumed the business must have closed down. 'Oh wow, that was fast. I'll head down that way to say hello. Thank you.'

'Anytime,' she replied, passing the coffee cup over the counter.

Joanna walked out of the busy shop and headed for the end of the main street. She sipped her coffee and was pleasantly surprised. Coffee orders were always risky in the bush, especially in a town as small as this one. Her stomach rumbled, and she hoped the Mattazio's store was open so she could buy herself something for breakfast, the cake in the coffee shop was not going to cut it.

Chapter Seventeen

Emily walked on the treadmill at the gym and thought about her last week. She had finalised two divorces and wasn't shocked to see the reasoning behind each of them: infidelity. She had kept an eye on Spencer's social media posts and noticed his assistant Victoria more and more in each of his videos and photos. She had texted him while he was away with a screenshot and a question mark and he had replied with a laughing face emoji, and the words, 'Don't be so paranoid.'

Emily had never been into the gym when she was younger and was blessed with good genetics being as slim as she was, but had noticed over the last few years as she had got busier, that she was spending so much time sitting down working that she was feeling pain in her lower back. She had signed up to the gym and worked with a personal trainer on a routine that would help strengthen her lower back and alleviate some of the pain she was having, and she was pleasantly surprised after a few months when the pain had left her. She had continued the routines on and felt herself getting stronger and stronger to the point where she was now addicted, and she couldn't miss a day of working out.

She showered in the women's bathroom and got dressed, ready to start her day. She wore a dark grey pantsuit, which was one of her favourites, and blow dried her hair, brushed it and left it out for a change. She packed her gym gear into her bag and headed outside into the carpark when she noticed a woman walking towards her.

As she got closer, she realised that it was Amy Davidson, the women who had come to her asking for advice for her husband. She looked in terrible shape, as she could see her clothes were hanging off her already thin frame, and the jeans she wore were ripped on one knee and covered in dirt. She had been crying, and Emily could see the streaks of black mascara on her face.

'Amy?' she asked as she got closer. 'Are you ok?'

Amy walked right up to her, and she tried to step back but was met by her car. Amy was right in close, and her voice shook as she spoke in a whisper to her. 'He's dead, Emily. He's fucking dead.'

'Who's dead?'

'Bo! They killed him.'

Emily was taken aback. Amy's fantastical story about the mafia and undercover police seemed to be true. 'What? What do you mean?'

'He's dead. And now they're after me.'

'How do you know he's dead?'

Amy stepped back and looked around and then wrapped her arms around herself. 'The undercover policeman. His name is Miles Cook. He's playing both sides. He's in too deep. He killed Bo.'

Emily side-stepped. 'Whoa, wait. I'm not sure you should be telling me all of this, Amy. You need to take this to the police.'

'Don't you see? I can't! Miles said that if I go to the police, he will tell them I killed Bo.'

Emily looked around the carpark. It was clear she was in serious trouble and their first meeting had stuck with her. 'Come on. Jump in my car and we'll head to a café and chat.'

She took her to the Edithvale Bakery, a giant, old, heritage listed building down in the port. The place was thriving with morning customers, and she ordered them two coffees and then ushered her into a booth in the back corner. 'How do you know for sure he was killed?'

'I hadn't heard from Bo in two days. I left Ned with my mum and drove up near Griffith to see if I could find where he was. Turns out he had driven to Sydney to deliver drugs with Miles and had turned his phone off. Anyway, I finally got in contact with him as I got to Griffith, and he took me out for dinner.' She wiped tears from her eyes and her blew her nose. 'It was the last dinner we ever had together.'

'What happened next?'

Amy's face turned sour. 'Miles, the cop, turned up. They call him 'Squirrel' up there. Don't ask me why, I have no idea. Anyway, he turns up after our dinner saying he needed to take Bo for a drive. I put my foot down, saying I hadn't seen him in weeks, and that I was coming. In the end, he gave up and said yes.'

A young girl walked over with the two coffees and Emily thanked them as Amy continued when she walked out of earshot. 'He drove us out into the bush. I was so disoriented, I felt like we were miles away from town. We got to a small clearing and stopped, and Miles told me to keep my head down. He said Bo and him had a business deal. They both got out of the car, and I looked up. There were four older men in a black Mercedes, all talking with Bo and Miles. I tried to hear what they were saying, but it was dark. And then.' She stopped and looked at Emily in the eyes. 'And then Miles pulled out a pistol and shot Bo, right between the eyes.'

'Oh my god,' Emily replied, unable to contain her shock.

Amy nodded and wiped tears from her eyes again. 'The other men had guns as well. I saw Miles pointing at the car and talking with the men. He turned and walked back to the car, and I thought Ned is not losing his mother and father tonight. So, I ran. I ran as hard as I could.'

'How did you get away?' Emily asked.

'I thought we were a long way from anywhere, but turns out we were near a highway. A truck stopped and gave me a lift back to Griffith. And here I am.'

It hit Emily all at once. 'Amy, you need to go to the police. You could be in danger. This so-called undercover cop could be after you.'

Amy shook her head. 'I can't. I told you. When I was running through the bush, he was yelling out at me. I heard it. He said he'll frame me for Bo's murder. Said I'll go to prison for the rest of my life. He said who will they trust? Me or a cop? Ned isn't losing his mother as well.'

Emily didn't know what to do or how she could help. 'But what can I do? What can I do to help you?'

'I don't know. I don't know what to do. I just didn't know who to talk to about all of this. I feel like you're the only person I can trust. You're the only person that knows the whole story.'

After discussing their options further, Amy received a call from her parents about her son and had to leave the bakery. Emily sat in the bustling shop for a few more minutes and tried to collect her thoughts. Amy's partner had clearly been a part of this Italian gang, but had been killed for an unknown reason. And what was this undercover cop named Miles' involvement in all of this? It was clear that he had turned. The police would not be letting him commit murder, no matter how deep he had gotten.

She went into work and tried to busy herself and not think about her rollercoaster of a morning. Nigel had noticed she looked off and knocked on her office door. 'You okay?'

She looked at her lifelong mentor and wondered whether to talk to him about what she had just heard. She watched as he leaned in the doorway and decided that now was not the time. Amy was in serious trouble, and what she had told her was private. She would speak to Spencer about it when he got home from Canberra. She knew she could trust him, and him only. 'I'm fine,' she replied.

Chapter Eighteen

The grocery store was literally the last shop at the end of the strip. Beside it was a vacant paddock which had weeds waist high, and beyond that, the highway continued into the dense bushland toward Dubbo. The store looked tired, and the light green paint around the front windows was cracked and peeling. The corrugated iron veranda roof, which stretched over the footpath to the edge of the road, was rusted, and looked to house a family of pigeons going by the bird droppings which covered the concrete.

The automatic doors opened as she walked up to them, and she surveyed the building inside. It was like walking into a time capsule, like the corner grocers and milk bars she remembered going into as a kid when she grew up in Melbourne. There was a single register to her left, and only three rows of shelving, which seemed to stretch right to the back of the shop. Vegetables and cold goods were on the left-hand-side wall where the row of fridges was, and the rest of the products were on old wire rack shelving.

'Give us a sec!' came a voice from the back of the shop.

Joanna stood at the register with her coffee and notepad in hand, and all of a sudden felt a pang of nervousness. Nick had sent her out here to do this on her own. What did she know about being a detective? She had watched him work and his process and had briefly worked with one of the other detectives for a short time in Edithvale. She knew to just be kind and relatable, and ask as many questions as she thought would be possible without upsetting the family member.

A thin, elderly woman with neat grey hair tied up in a ponytail and glasses came out from behind the right-hand side shelving with a smile. 'Morning love, what can I do for you?'

Joanna froze for a split second and then flipped open her badge. 'Good morning, mam, I'm Detective Joanna Gray with the New South Wales police force. I was hoping to speak with a member of the Mattazio family?' Nick had advised her she could tell a little white lie during her trip. Saying the word detective out loud gave her the small rush of adrenaline she needed, and she felt ready to face whatever came her way.

The elderly woman stopped in her tracks, and her jovial expression turned sombre. 'You certainly can. I'm Marie Mattazio. Is this about Linda?'

Joanna looked back at the door. 'It is. Did you want me to come back when you have time?'

Marie walked behind her to the automatic doors. She switched them to shut and flipped the open sign to closed. 'I've got all the time in the world, detective. Come on out back.' She continued past Joanna and led her down the aisles to the rear of the shop and through the back door into a small house. They sat down at a table in the kitchen, and Marie made herself a cup of tea. 'So, what number detective are you looking into this?'

'I'm not sure entirely sure. I work with Sydney homicide and was tasked with looking back into the case.'

Marie looked down into her tea. 'Sorry, that was rude. It's just been so long without any news. So, what do you want to know?'

'Tell me about Linda. What was she like?'

Marie sipped from her tea and continued smiling, with her mind clearly in the past. 'Brilliant. She was a wonderful kid. Never caused a fuss. Had close friends, was a star at school, good at sports, top of her classes. She was the perfect daughter.'

Joanna could see her memory was still very fresh in her mind. 'And she had just finished her first year at university before it all happened?' She couldn't bring herself to say the words. 'Did you notice a change in her during those few final months?'

Marie placed her cup of tea on the table and looked down at it. 'I did. It all started when she met him. And it got worse from there. She just began to change. She wasn't my Linda anymore. She was his.'

'And who are you referring to?' she asked.

Joanna watched as Marie's face turned dark. 'Spencer Hartford. It wasn't bad enough that he murdered my girl. Now I have to see his smiling face all over my newspaper and telly. Wouldn't spit on him if he was on fire.'

'And you're sure Spencer Hartford did it?'

Marie pursed her lips. 'Who else would do that to my girl? The detective's back then called it 'a crime of passion.' You know I looked up what that meant? It means that the perpetrator commits an act against someone because of a strong impulse of anger or jealously rather than premeditation. My girl was strangled to death, detective. And I never saw Spencer Hartford again. He didn't even attend her funeral. And they were supposedly in love. You tell me if those are the actions of an innocent man?'

Joanna listened intently and formulated her next question. 'When was the last time you saw Spencer?'

'A few days before she was killed. He came into the shop to see her, and we spoke for a short moment.'

She scrawled notes on her notepad. 'And did anyone else you know of have any problems with her?'

'No. No-one at all. Everybody loved her.' She sipped from her tea again. 'Any reason in particular that you are here? Detectives couldn't pin it on him back then. And unless there's new evidence, I doubt you'll be able to pin it on him now.'

Joanna tried her best to explain without saying everything. 'We believe something may have, uh, happened to somebody close to Mr. Hartford. We are trying to find anything in his past that may be able to explain his behaviour.'

Marie looked at Joanna. 'Has he killed again?' She started to laugh. 'I knew this would happen. I could feel it. Another family has lost someone. All because you lot couldn't pin it on him last time. You guys drove my husband to an early grave, now there is more blood on your hands.'

Joanna felt like she had been slapped across the face. 'I'm sorry Mrs. Mattazio, like I said, we are trying our best. I hope to give you some more answers soon.'

After wishing Marie all the best, she left the grocery store and walked back in the direction of the motel, feeling stupid. She wasn't prepared for the visceral reaction she got from Marie Mattazio and wanted to ring Nick and call this whole thing off. Her phone rang in her hand, and she looked at her screen, which read an unknown number from Sydney, and she answered it. 'Hello, Joanna Gray, speaking?'

'Morning Joanna, Chief Inspector Mark Johnson here.'

She sat down at one of the tables in front of the bookshop café and tensed up. She had never personally spoken with the chief inspector before and guessed he was the highest-ranking officer she had ever spoken to.

'Morning Chief Inspector. How can I help?'

'Mark's fine, Joanna.' She felt more at ease now they were on a first name basis. 'Nick tells me you're in Smith's Creek. Is it still as quiet as I remember?'

'It sure is. Not a lot going on here.'

'Unfortunate. I love those little towns. Are the Mattazio's still there?'

'Yes. I've just left their store.'

'How's Marie and Paulo?'

'Marie's good. Paulo passed away.'

She could hear inaudible speaking at the end of the line. 'Sad to hear. He was a nice fella. How did your chat with Marie go? What do you think?'

'Well, after reading the evidence and listening to Marie speak, I'd say Spencer Hartford is still top of the list. There doesn't seem to be anyone else that had a problem with her back then. And he never even attended her funeral. Can you believe that?' She used Marie's comments to her advantage. 'It sounds like a crime of passion to me.'

'Astute observation,' the chief replied. 'I have some good news.'

'What's that?'

'I have called the state evidence archives and got them to pull out the evidence we uncovered from the Mattazio crime scene. They've got some pieces of her clothing still and are going to re-test it for DNA. Obviously, we have made some incredible enhancements over the last twenty years in DNA testing. They will get the samples and re-test them against our database. Fingers crossed we get good news. This could be over a lot quicker than I thought.'

'But do you have samples for Spencer Hartford?'

'No, I don't. I'll have to leave that up to you and Nick to try and sort out.'

'Okay. Is there anything else?'

'Yes. She had a best friend called Katie. Can't remember her last name. Ask around and see if she's still in town. I never got a chance to speak with her, as her mother was sick with cancer. I think she had just died around the time of the murder.'

'Will do.'

They ended their call, and she felt a swell of pride again. The chief inspector of N.S.W homicide was calling her and giving her work. She made her way back to her room at the motel to do some more research in the case files, and after another hour of reading the file notes, felt her stomach rumble. She realised she hadn't eaten breakfast and decided to head into the pub to see what the food was like.

The pub was a busier than the night before and she noticed the tables in the bistro were half full. Waitresses walked from table to table with meals and drinks for the hungry patrons and as one walked past with a bowl of chips and gravy, she felt herself salivating at the thought of a hearty meal. She walked up to the bar again and noted the two old men were in their usual positions. Wes, the barman, was talking to them and she thought before lunch she might ask if he knew anything about this Katie girl. He looked to be in his 40s. Maybe he was a born and bred local, she wondered.

'She's back,' the first old bar fly commented in her direction. 'And looking better than ever.'

Joanna pulled her badge out of her pocket and flipped it open quickly. She looked in Wes the barman's direction. 'Sorry, I didn't formally introduce myself last night. Detective Joanna Gray. Was hoping I could ask you a few questions?'

She watched the two old men who were jeering both turn and look back down into their beer glasses and couldn't help herself. 'What? Don't want to talk to me anymore?'

'Not so tough now, are ya' boys?' Wes said with a chuckle. 'Of course, detective. What's this about?'

'I was looking for a friend of Linda Mattazio's from back in the day. Her name is Katie. Not sure of last name.'

Both of the old men turned back to her now with a curious expression, and she watched as Wes smiled. 'I know a Katie who was friends with Linda from back then. Her last name is Povich.'

'You do? She still in town?'

Wes chuckled. 'She is. She's in the kitchen out back right now. She's my wife.'

Chapter Nineteen

Nick sat in his car in the driveway of the Hartford residence and waited until Bec was walking up to the front porch before he opened his door. When Bec had bought flowers for Emily's parents and wanted to drop them at Spencer's house, he knew now was his time. He had never had to do it this way, and as he eyed the back of Bec, he looked around, hoping not to see anyone watching what he was about to do. The chief had notified him of the DNA samples being re-tested and had tasked him with getting a sample of Spencer's DNA without his detection. He knew it was going to be tough, but he had to try.

Nick could hear Bec's knock on the door and the sound of her and Spencer conversing as he reached the bins. He opened the lid of the dark green general rubbish bin and found what he was looking for almost immediately. There was a purple-coloured bag half open inside which was filled with food scraps, and he eyed a blue mug which he had seen Spencer holding when they were at the home on his first visit. It would be perfect. He used a plastic clip lock bag with his hand inside and scooped the mug out, which looked like it had been dropped as the edge of the handle was broken off it, and clipped it up inside the bag. He waited at the edge of the house and peeped out toward the front to see Bec still standing on the porch, and then hustled back to the safety of his car. He would submit the mug for DNA testing straight away. The chief could get top priority on it, and it would soon be at the top of the queue.

Later that day, the back beer garden of the Edithvale hotel was a hive of activity. A popular local band was slated to play later in the afternoon and the front bar was already full of patrons ready for the fun. Nick sat and watched Bec as the waitress took her order and could see the toll Emily's passing had put on her. The shellac on her nails on her right hand had been chewed and chipped, which was a sure sign she was feeling stress. Her hair was tied up in a messy bun and she had dark rings under her eyes from the lack of sleep.

Bec turned back from the waitress and looked at him with concern. 'You okay?' she asked.

That was the best part about her. She was always thinking about others; he thought. 'Yeah. You shouldn't be worried about me. I'm worried about you. You look like you've been through the wringer.'

'I have. Em's parents came to the house shortly after you left. I don't know if I've ever cried that hard in my life. Where did you head off to, anyway?'

Nick tensed in his seat. He didn't want Bec knowing what he was up to and needed more time. 'Got some more word on the Coleambally murder. Chief wanted to speak with me.'

Bec placed her hand on his. 'I know this is hard for you. I know it's hard to switch off.'

Nick felt terrible not telling Bec what he was really up to. But he wouldn't rest until he knew he had the truth. He knew he needed to get her some real answers. 'I'm sorry. I know. It's this job. It's my life.'

The waitress walked over and placed a glass of wine in front of Bec and a lemon squash in front of him. 'How long's it been since your last drink now?' Bec asked.

'Four months,' he replied. Sitting in this beer garden in the nice weather, coupled with the amount of stress he was currently under, would've been prime time for him to indulge. He watched a table of tradies beside him, all clinking their glasses together and drinking pints of beer. His tongue tingled in longing for the amber liquid.

'I'm so proud of you, babe. I could never do it.'

Nick sighed. 'I needed to. It would've put me in an early grave.'

Their meals soon followed, and he tucked into a giant chicken parmigiana. Bec picked at her chicken Caesar salad slowly without much interest. The meals were huge in this famous pub, and he left nearly half of the chicken on his plate. 'You want some of this?' he asked her, pointing down at the plate.

'No thanks.'

Nick decided now was the time. 'So, Emily never spoke to you about anything? Anything that would make you think that she would do this?'

Bec shook her head. 'No. I mean, she's always been a little melancholic. She and Spencer tried to have kids for a while back there, did IVF and all. But it never took.'

'Oh really? I didn't know that.'

As he finished his sentence, he noticed Bec tense at the sight of someone. He turned and looked back at the entrance of the beer garden to see Spencer standing beside a tall blonde woman, who looked to be in her early 30s. They were concealed by one of the brick columns that supported the courtyard roof, and it looked like Spencer hadn't noticed them until the waitress began making her way in their direction. Nick studied his face carefully as he eyed the pair, and noticed visible shock when he saw Bec.

Nick yelled out in their direction. 'Hey Spencer, over here!'

Bec kicked him under the table. 'Don't!'

Nick noticed Spencer's expression when he saw them. Who was this woman he was with? He looked like he'd been caught out in an awkward spot, and he knew it. He told the waitress they would find their own table, and the pair walked in their direction.

'Hey guys,' Spencer said.

'Hi,' Bec replied.

Nick's radar was on high alert. Something was up. 'Aren't you going to introduce us?'

The woman beside Spencer was absolutely stunning. She looked like a supermodel. Tall and rake thin, with tanned skin, perfect blonde hair and green eyes. She held a hand out in his direction. 'Hi, I'm Victoria, and you must be the famous Nick Vada?'

Nick shook her hand. 'Hi Victoria.' He pointed over in Bec's direction. 'This is my partner, Bec.'

Bec did that grin people do when they close their mouth and grin, with nothing in their eyes. He could see she was uncomfortable, and his radar was turned up to 10. There was something she wasn't telling him.

'Hi Bec. Nice to meet you. Spencer told me a lot about you.'

'Hi,' Bec replied flatly.

Spencer looked at him. 'Victoria's my assistant. You've been with me, what, eight months now?'

Victoria batted her eyelids in his direction. 'Nine.'

Spencer laughed. 'Wow. Nearly a year already. Anyway, we'll leave you guys to it. We're having a quick lunch to discuss some work issues and then I'm heading back home. I'll see you at the house later, Bec?'

'See you then.'

The couple walked away to the far booth in the corner of the beer garden and slid in together. He couldn't help but watch Victoria as she walked away. There weren't many women that looked like that in the bush.

'You like what you see?' Bec asked in a condescending tone.

Nick held both of his hands up. 'Hey. I'm not the one doing the wrong thing here.' He pointed with his fork in their direction. 'You mind telling me what the hell that was? Should he really be worried about work right now?'

Bec sipped from her wine and sighed. 'Emily had been speaking to me about it. She thought that he was sleeping with his assistant.'

'What do you think?'

'Well, they look pretty comfortable together. And I stalked his Instagram. She's in all of his photos. Some look pretty bad.'

'Why didn't you tell me?'

Bec shrugged. 'Because I knew exactly what you would think. You never liked Spencer from the start, Nick.'

Nick looked at her and felt a frustration he never had before. 'Bec, your best friend is dead. And now you tell me you think Spencer might have been cheating on her? Don't you think this is all a little bit suspicious?'

He could see that she was angry, as her brow furrowed and her voice rose. 'What do you mean, suspicious? Not everything is a murder investigation, Nick!'

The table of tradies beside them turned to look as she yelled. 'Hey, keep your voice down,' he replied.

'No! Unless you're trying to tell me Spencer killed her, I don't really know what you're implying!'

He looked at her and could see her anger. But knew she needed to hear it. 'That's exactly what I'm implying.'

Bec's mouth opened in shock. 'Just leave it, Nick. Drop it! She was depressed. There is no conspiracy. Not everything is a murder investigation. Can't you just be there for me? Please.'

'Bec, but..'

She cut him off. 'Oh, for god's sake. I'm done with this conversation.' She stood up so quickly that her chair tipped over backwards. 'I'm leaving.'

Chapter Twenty

Joanna waited for the busy lunch time rush to subside before she bothered Wes again. She sat and ate a perfectly cooked Lamb cutlet and drank a Diet Coke, while thinking back to her time with Nick and the way he had drank during their last case together. She made a mental note to keep an eye on him when she got back to Edithvale. The drink seemed to be his only vice.

A woman who looked to be around Wes's age walked in her direction. She was slim, with brown hair in a pixie cut. She wore a neat black apron that had 'The Smith's Creek Hotel' printed across the front of it and smiled in Joanna's direction as she got closer. 'May I sit?' she asked.

'Be my guest,' Joanna replied.

She held out her hand. 'I'm Katie Povich, Wes' wife, nice to meet you.'

Joanna shook it and replied, 'Nice to meet you, too. I'm Detective Joanna Gray, from N.S.W homicide.'

'Is this about Linda?' Katie asked.

'It is.'

'Did you finally get enough evidence to nab him?'

Joanna knew what her next answer would be, but still played dumb. 'Who?'

Katie laughed. 'You lot are all the same. Spencer Hartford.'

'We are still investigating, Katie. I've been sent to re-interview everyone who is still around. My records show that you were never spoken to back then?'

Katie shook her head. 'No. My mum passed away with cancer right around the time Linda was murdered.'

'I'm sorry to hear that.'

'It's okay. It was hard going for a while there. She had been sick a long time, and I cared for her. She died the same day Linda was found.'

'It must have been a tough time for you.'

'Oh, you have no idea. I was a wreck.' She looked over in the direction of the bar to her husband. 'I was just lucky I had Wes. He was there for me. He was like my rock. I'll always love him for that. Have you got a partner, detective?'

'No.'

'Well, make sure when you find a man that he's 100 per cent dedicated to you. There are a lot of men out there who will only want you for one thing. But there are some diamonds out there.' She looked in Wes' direction. 'Sometimes you've just got to polish them a little.'

'What do you remember of Linda?'

'Linda, Linda, Linda. Oh, she was brilliant. Smart, caring, she had time for anyone.'

'I've heard that from a few people now.'

'You have no idea. She was the best.'

'So, is there anything that you felt back then you could've told the police? Anything out of the ordinary? Was there something particular about Spencer Hartford that made you feel that way?'

Katie shrugged. 'Look, why we all think this is mostly due to what happened after. We never saw him again. Never spoke to him. He didn't even come to her funeral. What kind of person would do that? I thought we were friends. I got the feeling he was a very jealous person.'

'What makes you think that?'

'Oh, just a couple of things. One time at the Dubbo show, Wes rode in a ride with Linda and I rode with Spencer. Wes and Linda were chatting and having fun and he cracked it and ran off. We were kids, though. Some blokes are just like that.'

Joanna scrawled notes on her notepad. 'Did anyone tell any of this to the police back then?'

'No idea. We were all just so shocked. The police flew in here and were all over the place. It was so long ago.'

'When was the last time you saw Spencer Hartford?'

Katie's face turned sour. 'Out front of the Dubbo cinema. We hadn't caught up again after the whole debacle at the show. I reckon Linda was keeping him away from us. But this time he cracked it big time. That was when I told Linda she should try and break it off with him. That was her biggest fault, though. She thought she could fix everyone.'

'Why did he crack it?'

Katie thought for a moment. 'I don't remember. It was something to do with Wes. He always had an issue with him for some reason.' She looked over at the line at the bistro that had seemed to double since their conversation had begun. 'I'm sorry. I better get back to it. Looks like the lunchtime rush hasn't stopped just yet.'

'Thanks Katie. Can I grab your phone number? If I find out anymore, you will be the first to know.'

Katie scrawled her mobile phone number on the base of her notepad. 'Thank you for trying to help. Marie deserves answers.'

Joanna left the bistro and headed back to her room just as the sun was beginning to set. The rain in the morning that had seemed set in for the day had passed with barely a whimper. She placed the bottle of wine she had bought from Wes over the bar into her mini fridge, sat back down, and opened her laptop.

After a few minutes of research into the Hartford family, she found a profile on Spencer that was written in The Weekly Times two years earlier that answered most of the questions she was after. His parents, Mark and Lara Hartford, were generations old stock farmers, and were one of the wealthiest families of farmers in the state. Their homestead,

Hartwood, was heritage listed, and Joanna looked at the century old building in awe. It was stunning.

She scrolled further down the page and stopped in shock. Mark and Lara Hartford had been killed instantly in a car accident 15 years earlier on their way home from Sydney on the Hume highway. Spencer's only remaining family member was his younger sister, Lisa, who now resided in London as a commercial property lawyer. There was a family photo at the bottom of the page of them when they were younger. She resembled him in a way, the same high cheekbones, the same smile, the one that smelt of wealth. She looked almost insincere, like she knew she was better than you. Joanna had seen that look before. Reading further into the article, one comment took her by surprise where Spencer spoke of his estrangement with her, and used the words, 'Irreconcilable differences.'

She typed Lisa's name into Google and trawled through the websites. Nick had told him this was all top secret and that she needed to be as quiet as possible. But Lisa was in London, thousands of miles away, and didn't seem to be on speaking terms with Spencer, anyway. She wondered whether she should try and contact her, and ask about that time. She thought it best to call Nick for and ask permission.

Nick answered on the first thing. 'Hey. How's it going up there?'

'Much better than I expected.'

'Oh yeah?'

'Yep. Marie Mattazio, Linda's mother, still runs the local grocery store. Spoke to her, and she fully believes Spencer Hartford was guilty. Get this, he didn't even attend the funeral.'

'Shit. I didn't know that.'

'Yeah. And also, the chief said she had a best friend that he had never spoken to back then. Katie Povich. Turns out she owns the local pub I'm staying at.'

Nick laughed. 'Sometimes these small towns make it easy.'

'Yeah. I just spoke to her. She said Spencer was the jealous type. Flew off the handle at Linda in front of her a few times.'

'Hmm. It's all lining up. But without any concrete evidence. There's not much more we can do.'

'I'll keep looking. I was thinking about speaking with his sister. Lisa Hartford. She's a lawyer in London.'

'I wouldn't. What if she calls Spencer?'

Joanna outlined The Weekly Times article about Spencer and their estrangement and waited for Nick's reply. 'Okay. I mean, what's the worst that could happen? He won't know that you and I are connected in any way. We should be fine.'

Nick outlined what he had found out so far about Spencer, including his meeting with Victoria, his assistant at the pub, and then told Joanna she was doing a good job and wished her good night. Joanna ended the call, feeling a swell of pride. Her first day on the job as a detective had gone well. And Nick seemed happy. This week had been the breath of fresh air that she had needed.

She found Lisa's phone number through her LinkedIn profile and checked the time difference in London. It would be 8am over there, and she imagined her at the gym, or in preparation for her working day. She dialled the number and listened down the end of the line. After no answer, she left a message for her to call her back and then found her email address and began to type.

Lisa,

My name is Senior Constable Joanna Gray, and I am investigating the murder of Linda Mattazio. I would like to arrange a time to speak with you regarding this matter. Please call me anytime on 0400 540 946.

Thank you.

Chapter Twenty-One

Nick awoke the next morning in his motel room and was surprised to see Bec was still not back. He checked his phone to no new messages or calls and got up and rubbed his eyes. He messaged her and asked where she was and watched the screen. The three small dots that indicated someone was typing popped up and then disappeared. She clearly was not ready to talk.

He fossicked around in his bag and found his running gear. Ever since he was off the alcohol, he had felt a new lease on life. His clothes fit him better, his skin felt clearer, even the persistent nightmares that had haunted him for the past few years had seemed to deteriorate. He put his running gear on and heading outside to his car to grab his runners. He put his Apple Air Pods in his ears, set his classic rock playlist up, and set off toward the river.

His pace was steady, and he wasn't breaking any records, but when he hit his first kilometre, he felt clearer in his mind than he had all week. All of the puzzle pieces lay before him like a jigsaw. He just needed to put them all together in his mind.

After seeing Spencer with his assistant Victoria, it was plain to see to him that they could be an item. Along with Bec confirming Emily's suspicions of an affair, it was more than enough motive to want someone dead. Maybe Emily had confronted Spencer, and he had decided that enough was enough. That his new life with Victoria could be better in some way?

Nick reached the furthest point of his run and turned back toward the main street. He thought of Joanna out in Smith's Creek and their phone call the night before, and remembered to give the chief a call to comment on her good work. He decided she would make a great partner and wanted to speak to the chief about putting her on full time if she was interested. He slowed as he neared the first café he had gone to with Bec earlier in the week and decided to grab a takeaway coffee. As he neared the front door, a woman came out looking behind herself and he nearly ran headfirst into her.

'Sorry,' he said.

The woman turned around, and he realised it was Sarah Navarro, the constable who had found Emily's body. She was in casual clothes and held a takeaway coffee cup and banana bread in her hand. 'Good morning.'

'Morning. How are you?'

'Good. Out for a run?' She held up her banana bread. 'Now you're making me feel guilty.'

Nick chuckled. 'Don't. You're young. You won't need to start running for a few years yet.' He realised now might be a perfect time to ask her about finding Emily. 'Hey, do you have a minute?'

Sarah looked down at her phone. 'Yeah, what's up?'

Sarah sat outside in the sunshine with her coffee while he ordered, and soon he returned with his coffee and the same banana bread in hand as he took a seat in front of her. 'Sorry, couldn't resist. It looks good.'

'So, what did you need?'

Nick knew he had to tread delicately. Any word to Greg Baseley about this and he knew Spencer would be on his case. He decided to try and play off Bec's curiosity as an angle. 'The Hartford scene. My partner Bec just can't get it out of her head. She's so upset.'

Sarah sighed. 'It wasn't great.'

Nick sipped his coffee. 'What did you see?'

'A call came in from a local delivery driver. Said he'd found a body. I got the call from dispatch over the radio and myself and Sergeant Jones headed straight there.'

'What time was that?'

'Early. About 9am. We got there quickly. The driver opened up the front door for us. He seemed shaken up. He knew her fairly well, apparently.'

'How was the house?'

'Clean, except for some leftover dishes in the sink and an empty wine glass and bottle on the island bench.'

'What about the dog?'

Sarah's eye focused away in the distance. 'That was the worst bit. The howl. I could hear it from the street. The dog was at the tree. Under her. Hadn't left her side.'

'How did you get her down?'

'We didn't. We went out to her, and Sergeant Jones tried to climb up to cut her down, but she was too high up. I called it in to the fire brigade. They came and cut her down.'

He knew that this was his moment. 'I went out and saw that tree. It's massive.'

Sarah nodded. 'It is.'

'Don't you think it's odd how she got up there?' he asked.

Sarah bit into her banana bread and chewed it quietly. 'That's what the sergeant said. But I'd seen her at the gym. She was as tough as they come. I just think she climbed up there and jumped.'

It was abit of a stretch; he thought. He had been to a few suicides by hanging in his time, and they were always a lot more elegant. A beam or a branch. A chair and a rope. No one ever jumped. What if the rope broke? He knew not to push the issue. 'Hmm. Fair enough.'

'When's the funeral?' Sarah asked.

Nick realised he hadn't asked Bec that yet. He needed to get to the bottom of this before they buried her. In case they needed to retrieve further evidence. 'I'm not sure.'

'It's just so sad. She was so young.'

They continued chatting for a while about rural policing and some of the high points of Nick's career. He got the feeling that she may have been abit of a super fan. His exploits were well known, especially in Edithvale, which was only one town over from his hometown, and he was used to being recognised when people saw him.

Nick headed back to his motel room, showered and got dressed for the day. Joanna text him to say she didn't think there was much more she could glean from Smith's Creek, and he advised her to pack it up and head back here to Edithvale. He walked down to the reception and booked the room beside him for her, knowing that she was going to need a place to stay until they got to the bottom of this. He got into his car and made his way towards the Edithvale police station when the chief rang.

'Morning.'

'Morning,' he replied.

'How's it going?'

'Slowly. I went to the morgue and spoke with the coroner. She died from the hanging, but she had scratches all over her arms, which look an awful lot like defensive wounds. Also, she was drugged to the eyeballs and drunk.'

'None of that proves anything, though.'

'It doesn't. But, I ran into the delivery driver who found her just before my morgue visit. I asked him what he saw when he found her. Nothing, no chair, no ladder. God knows how she got in that tree.'

'Not a nice way to go,' the chief replied.

'No, not at all. Guess what? I ran into Spencer at the morgue.'

'Shit. I told you to lie low.'

'It gets better, chief. He asked me to look into it, into why she died.'

'Wow. I didn't expect that.'

'Maybe it's a keep your friends close and your enemy's closer type of deal?'

'Maybe. It's ballsy I'll tell you that. If he is guilty, I certainly wouldn't be out tempting you. I'm sure he knows who you are, and what you've solved.'

It was a compliment, which wasn't something he usually got from the chief, and he took it. 'Thanks, but I'm still far off. He was in Canberra the night before her death, apparently, and unless he was in two places at once, I won't be able to pin it on him. I'm going to call Hattie this morning and get her to pull his phone records.'

'Well, that sounds like your next step,' the chief replied. 'Spoke with Joanna last night.'

'Oh yeah?'

'Yep. She's done good work up there at Smith's Creek. Found a friend of Linda's I could never get. We need to look into keeping her on if she's interested.'

'I agree.'

Nick hung up the call and walked into the Edithvale police station. There was a new cop on the reception desk, and he gave him a curt nod as he walked past. He headed up to the interview room that Greg Baseley had given him to use and set out looking into what Spencer was up to the night of Emily's death.

Nick checked Spencer's social media accounts and found what he needed straight away. Spencer had spoken at a conference outside of Canberra at a Young Farmers Association dinner the night of Emily's death. He watched him speak to the hundreds strong crowd and spotted Victoria in the back of the frame smiling and waving as the speech ended. He really didn't seem to care as he placed his hand on the small of her back and waved to the crowd. They looked like members of the royal family.

He Google mapped the location of the function centre back to Edithvale, and decided that it was totally possible to make the trip back at night and return back to Canberra under the cover of darkness still. It was only a 4 and a half hour drive, and his speech was at 5pm. It was more than enough time.

His next post on his Facebook was an image inside a motel room with the location pinned as the Adina Canberra, with an image of a TV screen with his face on it. This type of fame still seemed new to him, it seemed. He dialled the number of the Adina Canberra and kindly asked them for assistance in solving a murder investigation, all while doing his best to mention nothing of Spencer. Some places clamped up immediately and began sprouting the words they heard on TV about warrants and the like, but the manager he spoke to was professional and easy going. He emailed through the camera files of the carpark and hotel lobby that Nick requested within an hour, and he emailed them directly to Joanna to give her a new task when she arrived back in town.

His next step was to call Hattie Boyd, the homicide squad's resident tech analyst. As usual, she answered on the first ring, in her thick European accent. 'Morning detective.'

'Morning Hattie, you looking after the chief?'

She giggled. 'Always. You ever coming back to visit me?'

'I'd like to. But too much happening out in the bush. I've never liked the city anyway.'

'Well, we are opposites in that regard,' she replied.

'Hey, got an easy job for you.'

'What's that?'

'Spencer Hartford. You heard of him?'

'Yes. Liberal member for Farrer. Slated to be our next water minister if he plays his card right, they're saying.'

He wasn't surprised she knew of him. 'Not much gets past you, does it?'

'It's good to keep up with what the government is doing, Nick. It's more important than what you think. Now, what about Spencer Hartford?'

'I need you to track his phone, if possible, over the last two weeks. I need cell tower locations. I'm not too fussed in regard to calls and messages. I just need to know where he has been.'

Nick heard the sound of the keyboard clacking furiously. 'On it.'

As Hattie ended their call like a dog with a bone, he heard a knock on the door and looked up to see Greg Baseley walk in. 'Howdy, how's it going on here?'

'Slowly.'

He held a mug of coffee in his hand and casually sat down on the opposite side of his desk. 'Yeah?'

'Yeah,' he replied. Unsure of the inspector's visit.

'Had a chat with Paul McNaughton at the RSL club last night.'

His shoulders dropped. He should've known that Paul would've spoken to him. Relationships in the bush and trust were paramount. 'Oh yeah? What'd he say?'

Greg placed his mug on the table. 'He said you went in to look at Emily Hartford's body. Said you were asking all types of questions. What the hell is going on?'

Nick knew the jig was up. The chief trusted the inspector, so he knew he had to go out on a limb and drop the bombshell to someone. 'I was. I think Emily Hartford was killed.'

The silence in the small interview room was deafening. And he watched Greg sizing him up. 'Okay then. I didn't expect that. What makes you think that? That's quite a serious accusation you're making.'

'I'm sorry I didn't say anything earlier. It just stinks, Greg. Did you see the scene? The Oak tree she was under was huge. There's no way she would've climbed up there and done it like that. Have you ever seen anyone wrap a rope around their neck and jump to commit suicide? Not to mention the fact that she was drugged to the eyeballs and drunk. I also ran into Manny, the delivery driver who found her. No chair, no ladder, nothing. How'd she get up there?'

Greg nodded. 'Paul told me her alcohol content was three times the limit.'

'Yep.'

'So, million-dollar question. Who do you think killed her?'

Nick placed his hands on the table. 'It's pretty obvious, isn't it? Spencer Hartford.'

Greg sipped from his mug. 'I had a read of the Mattazio case file last night. Now I know why you're looking into it. I remember it now from back when it happened. But I never knew about Spencer. It doesn't look good.'

'That's where Senior Constable Gray is. I sent her up to Smith's Creek to re-interview some friends and family. You know Spencer never even attended the funeral? If they were so in love, why wouldn't he go to the funeral?'

'I don't know,' Greg replied, lost in thought. 'But why would Spencer do this? I know what most politicians are like, and he's not like them. He's smarter. What did he have to gain?'

Nick opened his phone and spun the screen around to the inspector, who watched the video of Spencer and Victoria side by side, waving to the adoring crowd.

Greg leaned back in his chair and sighed. 'Money or love is always the motive. That's what the old detectives used to say.'

'I'd say this one is love,' he replied.

Chapter Twenty-Two

Linda finished serving the last customer for the day and began to close up the shop. She dragged the front trolleys full of fresh fruit through the front door and quickly wiped down the bench tops. She had to rush, as Katie planned on picking her up at 6pm for their trip to Dubbo to go to the movies.

She had made up with Spencer after their argument at the show and had had a pleasant few weeks together whenever he found the time to get to Smith's Creek. She didn't have a car, so she relied on him to make the trip, and he had managed to sneak away from his parents' farm a few times so they could sneak away to spend as much time together as they needed.

She hadn't re-introduced him to her friends yet, and was wary to, as he had made a few odd comments since their first argument back at the show in their last few meetings. It was clear he had an issue with Wes, and he would busy himself when they were together asking questions about their past relationship. She tried her best to quell his jealousy, explaining that it was just a childhood romance, and that they hadn't even kissed, but he seemed more and more adamant that something was going on between them, and it was starting to frustrate her.

In her bedroom, she stood in front of her mirror applying lipstick and some blush, and stood back to admire her handiwork. She looked good enough for a trip to the movies, she thought, plus it was dark in there. She didn't need to be too dolled up. She grabbed her handbag and placed her wallet and lipstick in it and had a sudden brain wave. On her way out the front door, she would grab some M&M's and lollies from the front of the shop. That way she and Katie could save some money, instead of paying the hiked-up prices of the confectionary at the movies.

Her mum popped her head into her room. 'What time will you be home, love?'

Linda looked at her watch. 'It's at least a 45-minute drive home, mum. Probably late.'

'Alright. Please be careful.'

Hearing the honk of the car horn out front, she knew it was her cue to leave. 'That's Katie, mum. Love you!' She ran down the central aisle, and slowed at the lolly section, swiping two bags of M&M's and some red liquorice, which was Katie's favourite. She re-arranged the shelving again, so it looked like nothing had moved, and ran on out the front doors. With her mother popping in to talk to her, she didn't realise it at the time, but she had forgotten her mobile phone back in her room.

Katie was lucky in one aspect. Due to her mum being so sick, she was given her car, which was a brand new, black Holden Commodore with a rumbling V8 engine. Linda didn't know much about cars but enjoyed the looks that they got around town when they drove in it together.

She jumped into the passenger seat. 'Hey you.'

'Hey yourself, ready for a movie night?' Katie replied.

She smiled. 'Of course. I love a girl's night.'

Katie turned the car out and cleared her throat. 'Ahh that. About that.'

'What?'

'I, ah, invited Wes to come with us. Hope that's ok?'

She punched her in the arm. 'What are you up to! Cheeky bugger.'

Katie grinned. 'I don't know. I guess just these past few months have had me realising that he's a pretty cool guy.'

She laughed. 'He really is. You two would make a great couple! I wish I had known. I could've brought Spence along for a double date.'

Katie was quiet for a beat. 'Yeah. Shame.'

She looked at her. 'What?'

Katie shook her head. 'It's nothing, Linds. Don't you just think that he acted like abit of a dickhead at the show? I mean, you've known Wes since you were in kindergarten. There was no reason to act like that.'

She chuckled. 'Yeah, he got a bit shitty. It's fine though, it just means he cares.'

'Whatever you say,' Katie replied.

Katie stopped at Wes's home, which was directly behind the Smith's Creek fuel service station to pick him up and then the trio headed for Dubbo. It was a clear night, and the road was empty, and as the three friends spoke about life, Linda could already feel the spark in the air, and the buzz of fresh love, as she listened to Katie and Wes speak to each other.

She should've seen it coming. When she left for university, they were two of the last people of their high school class left in town; it was inevitable that they would get together.

Linda opened her bag, fairly certain that she would have a text message from Spencer that would need replying too. He would text her every few hours, and she would be met with text messages of question marks if she didn't get back quickly. She rummaged through her bag and pulled out item by item. 'Shit. I think I left my phone at home.'

'Don't stress. You can use mine if you need,' Katie replied.

'It's not that. It's Spencer. He likes to know where I am.'

'He sounds pretty intense,' Wes replied from the back seat.

She turned back to him. 'Nah. He just cares.'

'What's he doing tonight, anyway?' Katie asked.

'Out for dinner with his parents in Dubbo.'

'Well, maybe we'll see him!' Wes said with a laugh.

Linda sat through the movie, which Katie failed to mention again was Wes' choice, a sci-fi movie called I-Robot, and was pleasantly surprised. Sci-fi wasn't her thing, but the movie had Will Smith in it, and she liked him as an actor, so it kept her engaged long enough that she didn't even notice Wes and Katie kissing beside her. As the credits rolled and the lights came up, she giggled at the sight of Katie's tussled hair and Wes' face, which had remnants of Katie's bright red lipstick on it.

'You've got a little something on your face,' she said with a laugh, handing Wes a tissue.

Wes went red himself and wiped his face with a sheepish grin. 'Thanks.'

They walked out of the movies, and Katie spoke to them both. 'Hey, why don't we get one more drink before we head home?'

Linda cautiously looked at her watch again and tried not to imagine the number of messages that Spencer would be sending her. 'It's getting late.'

'C'mon. Just one,' Katie said, 'Pleeease.'

Linda was easily convinced; she didn't want them to know she was stressed about Spencer trying to get onto her. 'Alright,' she said. They turned and walked along the footpath in the clear night on the busy street and she placed herself between the new couple and wrapped her arms around each of them and pulled them in tight. 'Plus. I think we need to celebrate the two lovebirds.'

The screech of car tyres shattered the quiet night air, and the trio spun around to see a Toyota Hilux ute stopped in the middle of the street. They heard the sounds of it being placed in reverse and it sped backwards and zoomed into a carpark just down from them.

The three jumped back and Wes said, 'Jesus, what's this guy's problem?'

Spencer was sitting in the driver's seat and beside him, his sister Lisa sat, both on their way home from a family dinner. He opened the driver's side door and slammed it with a violent thud, and stepped up onto the footpath with a face full of fury.

Linda looked at Wes and then Katie, who had a scared looked on her face and said, 'Give me a minute.'

He was dressed nicely in chinos and a checked button-up shirt and as she got closer, she could see he was angry. She smiled and went to grab his hand. 'Hey, sorry I..'

Spencer held his mobile phone out in her face and cut her off. 'I've been trying to call you for the last two hours! Where the fuck have you been?!'

'I'm sorry. I left my phone at home! I've been to the movies! Please, don't be mad.'

He looked over in Katie and Wes's direction. 'I can fucking see that. I see what's happening here. You're off with him having fun while I'm trying to get back in my mum and dad's good books. You've really fucked up this time, Linda.'

She turned back and looked at her friends, and was thankful they were out of earshot. 'Babe. It's not like that. Wes and Katie are an item. I tagged along for a movie. That's all.'

Spencer held up a hand. 'I don't want to hear it. I trusted you and you lied to me.'

'Spence, please.'

Katie walked up behind her, and she was sure she was coming up to try and diffuse the situation. 'Hey Spencer, you're looking spiffy tonight.'

His face turned from dark and sour to bright in an instant, and she was shocked at how easily he could change emotions. 'Hey Katie, how's your night been?' He pointed to his sister in his ute. 'Just had a family dinner.'

'Why don't you come have a drink with us? We were gonna' have one before we headed home.'

Spencer shook his head. 'Sorry. I can't. It's past my little sis's bedtime. Another time, yeah?'

Linda looked over to the ute and saw Spencer's sister give a meek wave. Katie walked back to Wes, and she wove her hand around Spencer's waist and kissed him in front of everyone. 'I love you, Spencer Hartford. There's no one else. You have nothing to worry about.'

Spencer smiled and returned her kiss. If he was still angry, he didn't show it. He wished her goodnight and hopped back in his ute. His sister was silent in the passenger seat, and it wasn't until they hit the main highway that she spoke. 'So that's the new girlfriend?'

Spencer shook his head. 'It was. Not for much longer, though.'

Chapter Twenty-Three

Joanna sat at the laptop, sipping her coffee, and watched the screen intently. There were multiple different camera setups from the motel carpark that they had sent to Nick, and she had already sat through 30 minutes of sped up footage for one of them and found nothing. She opened the next file and continued searching until she found it. 'Bingo,' she said out loud.

At 7:00pm, a black Mercedes Benz bearing the number plates, 'Hartford1' on them, slowed for the boom gate, and then continued on out into the night. She paused it and tried to see through the screen into the car window and couldn't make out a face. But the plate was clear. It was Spencer's car, and it was leaving right around the time Nick thought it would be leaving.

Nick walked into the room as she looked at the image of the car. 'Got something?'

Joanna turned the screen for him to view it better. 'Just like you said. That's his car. Leaving at 7.'

'That would put him in Edithvale around midnight.'

Joanna nodded. 'It works.'

Nick sat down beside her as she worked the toggle bars on the camera setup. 'Fast forward to 4:00am.'

Joanna clicked four times speed, and they waited. Only two more cars came through the screen at the time, along with a delivery van with food for the kitchen. At 4:00am they slowed it down to double speed and waited. At 5:15am he said, 'Stop. Slow it down.' As a bonnet of a black Mercedes Benz creeped into the frame. The boom gate stayed down, and they watched as the window buzzed down slowly. An arm came out with a swipe card and Spencer's face, which was clear as can be, came out of the window, concentrating on the screen. The boom gate opened, the taillights dimmed, and the car moved on forwards out of the frame.

'Well. This looks really bad,' Joanna replied.

Nick sat in silence, putting the pieces of the puzzle in his head together. The tree. The scratches on her arm. Her blood alcohol content. This vision. Joanna was right. It was all coming together.

'It does. I think we need to speak with Spencer Hartford officially,' he replied. 'Follow me.'

Nick walked out of the interview room with Joanna behind him and made his way down to Greg Baseley's glass office. He had a plate on his desk with his lunch, which looked like leftovers from the night before. 'Gee, this looks serious,' he said.

'Sorry Greg. We won't bother you on your break,' he replied.

Greg slid the plate toward his computer monitor and wiped his mouth. 'All good. What's up?'

Nick outlined everything they had previously spoken about and showed him the footage of Spencer leaving and re-entering the motel carpark. Greg sat still for a second and then looked up at him. 'What do you think?'

'I think we need to bring him in for a chat. I'll call the chief, though, get a second opinion.'

Greg agreed. 'Good idea. There'll be an absolute frenzy if the media hears about this. Have you got any traction on the Mattazio case?'

'Her friends and family seem adamant that he did it. But we have no new evidence that ties him to it. Joanna is waiting to hear back from his sister to see if she's any help. Apparently, they were estranged. Maybe she knows something we don't? Also, the chief has submitted her clothing again for DNA checks. And I've managed to get a sample out of his bin that may have a sample of his DNA on it. Fingers crossed; we might get a hit.'

Greg shook his head and grinned. 'You Sydney detectives are tenacious bastards. Nicking his rubbish, bloody hell. You could've just asked him.'

'And where would that have got me? He would've known we were onto him,' he replied.

Greg put both of his hands up. 'Hey, I'm not here to tell you how to do your job. You get results, no matter how controversial. If Mark Johnson agrees with you, be my guest. Chain of command and all.'

They left the inspector to his lunch and walked out of the station into the sunshine. Nick grabbed out his phone and dialled the chief.

'How's it going?'

Nick cut to the chase. 'Good. We've got footage of Spencer leaving his motel at 7am and returning to it at 5am the night Emily was killed. I want to bring him in for a chat. Let him sweat abit. See what happens.'

'Hmm. It's not a lot to go on. This could go wrong all sorts of ways. But if you think you can break him, go for it.'

'Any updates on the DNA?'

'Nothing yet. I called the state pathology lab. I've given them your number directly. Results should be back any time now.'

'Ok. Speak soon.'

'Good luck.'

They got into his car, and Joanna sat quietly. 'What do you think? he asked.

'It's your call,' she replied slowly.

He kept looking ahead and rubbed his eyes. 'If I do this. Bec is going to lose it. She told me to drop it. To leave it. I don't know what she'll say if she finds out I've kept at it.'

'He can't get away with it, though, Nick.'

'I know.' He started the car up. 'I know.' He idled slowly away from the police station and called Spencer's number.

'Nick, how are ya', mate?'

'Good Spencer, you home?'

'I am. You got news?'

'Sort of. I'll be over shortly.'

'See you then.'

They made the drive over towards the house, and he could feel Joanna tensing in her seat. He looked over at her. 'Relax,' he said. 'This is going to go one of two ways.' His black Mercedes was parked in the driveway, and they pulled in behind it. At the front of the house was a bright red Hyundai Veloster coupe, and he was sure he knew whose car it was going to be.

They got out and walked up to the front door. As Joanna went to knock, Spencer opened it up from inside and smiled at them both. He wore neat chino pants and a Ralph Lauren polo shirt with the collar pulled up. Nick introduced Joanna to him. 'Hey Spencer. This is Senior Constable Joanna Gray. She's been helping me for the past few days.'

Spencer held out of his hand, and she shook it. His smile was one of supreme confidence, and he watched the way he looked at her, with his full un-divided attention. It was an art that many politicians were yet to master.

'Spencer Hartford. Nice to meet you.'

'You too,' Joanna replied flatly.

Nick eyed Victoria walking down the hallway from behind him, and she walked up to say hello. 'Hi Nick, good to see you again.'

'Hi Victoria, this is Joanna.' As Joanna greeted her, he watched her flat expression turn to awe at the sight of her. She truly was a beautiful woman. Seeing her here standing beside Spencer, he decided to change tact, and tell a little white lie. He thought the bright lights of the police station might get the truth out of him. 'Hey, you got a minute?'

Spencer nodded and told Victoria he'll be in in a minute. He couldn't help himself as he watched the back of her in awe as she walked away. 'What's up?' Spencer replied.

'We've learnt some more about Emily's last few days. Thought it might be easier if you meet us down at the police station to go over it? We've got some footage as well.'

Spencer looked at him with suspicion and pointed to the camera above the door. 'It can't be them. They're broken. Been trying to get a tech out here for months to look at them. Although I think the Eagleton's behind us might have a camera in our yard, did you get footage from that?'

Nick made a mental note to get any footage that the neighbours might have. 'It's not that.'

Spencer shifted uncomfortably and looked at them both. 'Alright then. Shall I meet you there?'

Back in the car on the way back to the station, Joanna read his mind. 'I thought that would've been harder.'

'Me too. He's smart. He won't make it easy. We need to get that footage from the neighbours if they have it as well.'

'Yep. As soon as we are done with him, I can head over and grab it.'

Chapter Twenty-Four

Emily sat inside her office at work and tried to read through the court notes for her next defendant she was working with. She stood up and walked over to the window again for the third time that day and looked out onto the road. She swore she had seen the same black Ford Ranger ute parked in two separate spots near the front of her work, and she was beginning to feel scared.

Amy hadn't given her phone number, she had only given hers out, so she had no way to check in with her to see if she was ok. It had been three days since their meeting in the bakery and she was starting to really worry. She wanted to go to the police, but she remembered what Amy had said about the undercover policeman, and how he said he would frame her for her partner's murder if she spoke up. Her son couldn't afford to have no mum now his father was gone.

Emily opened her phone up to her Instagram app and watched Victoria's latest story. She was at a fancy café in Canberra with a friend, and she watched her talking about her smoothie and elaborate avocado smash she was eating. She hated her. She hated the way she spoke; she hated the way she looked. She remembered when Spencer introduced her to her in this very building. And she remembered how short her skirt was, and her tacky makeup. It was just like the shows she saw on TV. It was like she was being replaced by a newer, shinier model.

What was so wrong with her? She wondered to herself. She was slim, and surely fitter and stronger than her. She was a lawyer and had a great family. What else could he possibly want? They had never had many arguments or disagreements during their marriage, and she only noticed him slowly starting to distance himself when he was offered his new role in federal politics, and he began his commute back and forth to Canberra.

Victoria wasn't the first one, though. She remembered Jessica, a young local girl, who worked as his assistant when he was mayor in Edithvale. She remembered the way he would hungrily look at her and her revealing clothing, and how he would flirt openly with her in front of her. But Victoria was different. She was older. Closer to their age and seemed brighter than most. After watching their supposed working relationship blossom over the past few months, she was sure now with the way that Spencer was acting that they must be sleeping together.

The day dragged on, and she tried her best to concentrate, but at 4:00pm decided she'd finish early. She closed her laptop and stretched her arms over her head. Her shoulders were still sore from her morning workout, and she grimaced in pain as she picked up her heavy laptop bag and headed for the door.

'Night,' she said to the front receptionist. 'See you tomorrow.'

'Bye Em,' the receptionist replied with a warm smile.

She dialled Spencer's number when she got into her car and waited for him to pick up.

'Hey.'

'Hey, how's your day going?'

'Busy busy. Had a meeting with the water minister at parliament house which dragged out, now heading out to the young farmers' association to do a speech.'

'Oh right. Is Victoria with you?'

There was silence at the end of the line, and she heard a voice. 'Yeah, she is. She's giving me a hand with my speech.'

Emily cursed under her breath. There never seemed to be a moment they were apart these days. 'Oh. Ok.'

'Everything okay, babe?'

'Yeah. I'm fine. Heading home early. Going to chill out and have a quiet night.'

'Okay, well, I'll let you know how my speech went. Keep an eye out on the news. You might see me. Got to go.'

Emily heard the click at the end of the line, and she pressed the hang-up button on her car. Another speech, another dinner, more time for Spence to get to know Victoria. She missed him terribly. And wished she could rewind to five years ago when he was still working in town at the law firm with her. Times were much simpler back then.

She got home, turned the air conditioning on and jumped in the shower. Remi sat happily in the doorway of her ensuite on the cool concrete floor and watched on as she cleaned her hair and applied a face scrub. The warm water cascaded over her, and she felt all of her worries about Amy and Spencer leaving her as she cleansed herself. She was going to hang out with Remi and forget about her day, maybe have a glass of wine, and watch the next season of The Crown, which had just come out on Netflix.

She dressed in her grey pyjama pants, put a workout singlet on, and padded down to the kitchen to look in their wine cabinet in the pantry. There was a 2019 bottle of Penfold's Grange that Spencer had given her for her birthday, and she decided his plans of them enjoying it together weren't important anymore. If he was off cruising around Canberra with another woman, she would enjoy it herself.

The sun had set now, and she left the curtains up so she could still see out into the backyard. She loved seeing her garden lit up at night, with the pool looking perfect and the new fairy lights that she had just put up that ran around it and along the fencing, which continued all the way down to the Oak tree. It was her favourite view in the whole world, and it was a view she had worked really hard for. As she sat down on the couch, and Remi jumped up onto her lap, she scratched her under the ears and rubbed her cheeks, feeling appreciative of the company.

She looked at her phone beside her on the couch and wasn't surprised to see that Spencer hadn't called or text. She imagined him sitting in a nice restaurant with Victoria, drinking and laughing and both enjoying each other's company. He thought of Bec, her best friend, and thought maybe she should call her, talk about her problems, hash it out. But it was late, and she was busy with her new partner, a new love. She didn't need to be bothered.

The sound of her doorbell jolted her from her concentration on the TV, and Remi jumped up and barked. 'Remi. Settle,' she said. She got up, feeling confused, and told Remi to wait in the lounge. It was 8:00am. Who would be at her door at this time of the night? She opened her phone to look at her security camera app and swore to herself. Spencer was meant to get them fixed. She had been asking him for months, and he still hadn't got to it. She made a note to just do it herself tomorrow. She couldn't rely on him anymore.

Emily padded down her hallway and looked at the photos on the wall, reminiscing about happier times with Spencer. She missed him. She needed to take charge and fix it herself. She was still his wife. There was still time to fix this. The porch light was on, and she could see the outline of a dark figure standing at the front door. It wasn't until she turned the handle and cracked the front door that she remembered Amy and everything that was happening. She made a snap decision and went to close the door back but saw a black boot snap in between the door and jamb.

Emily jumped backwards as the door opened and stood dead still. Under the porch light was a tall man, dressed in all black, with a matching cap and a rough brown beard with grey streaks in it. He held a small black pistol in his hand and his eyes shone in the darkness. Suddenly, she knew she was in big trouble.

'Evening Mrs. Hartford. Can I come in?'

Chapter Twenty-Five

When Linda got home that night, she ran straight for her room. Her mobile phone was almost flat, and it vibrated as she picked it up, with fifteen missed calls and countless text messages. She read through each message as they got angrier and angrier and felt helpless. Why couldn't he see that she loved him? She didn't want anyone else. She especially didn't want Wes. He would see it, she would prove it, she would prove to him that she loved him, that they'd be together forever. She wasn't going to give up that easily.

The next morning, she busied herself setting up the shop, and kept her mobile phone beside the cash register, in case Spencer called or messaged. Her mum came down in her usual work outfit, dark jeans and a green t-shirt and an apron, and smiled at her. 'Good morning, Hun.'

'Morning.'

'You were home late.'

'I know. I'm sorry. Movies ran late.'

'You left your phone at home. I heard it buzzing in your room.'

Linda laughed. 'I know, sorry. Spencer was trying to call me.'

'When are we going to see this boy again? I thought we could invite him around for a family dinner?'

'I'd like that mum.' She thought about the way he had acted the night before again. He was really angry, but maybe a nice dinner might cheer him up. 'I might call him and ask.'

As the day wore on, she checked her phone constantly. She wasn't going to message or call him. She didn't want to break and message first. She didn't want to bother him. He needed to calm down first; she knew he would. She served the next few customers and was surprised at how busy the store was for a Thursday afternoon.

As one of her mother's friends walked on out of the store, she heard the buzz of her mobile phone on the countertop. She ran back to the register, pulled the aerial out and flipped it open, reading Spencer's name on screen. 'Hello?'

'Hey. I'm an hour away. Wanna go for a drive?'

'I'd love that,' she replied. She knew he would crack and be the one to contact first.

'See you soon.' He hung up abruptly, and she smiled. He might still be grumpy, but she knew exactly what would cheer him up.

Linda closed the store up as quick as she could, and let her mum know she was going out with friends. She wanted to get Spencer in the right mood before she broached the dinner subject with him. It might not be tonight, but it would be soon. She dressed casually, and when she thought it had been around an hour, walked out and locked the shop doors behind her. It was a beautiful night; the sky was amber red as the sun was setting, and she could hear the cockatoos calling in the distant gumtrees.

Soon, she saw Spencer's white Hilux ute coming down the main street. She walked down to the edge of the footpath and stuck her thumb out like she was a backpacker looking for a ride. Spencer slowed, and his passenger window buzzed down. 'Need a ride?' he asked.

'Sure.'

Spencer went out in the direction of the lovers' lane lookout out of town that they'd been driving out to to sleep together, and she knew what he had come for. If this is what he wanted, she thought, she would give it to him. She wanted him to be happy. They drove in silence for a few minutes without him saying another word, and she kept stealing a glance at his face, which was transfixed on the highway ahead. She could see how tightly he was gripping the steering wheel, and she thought he still looked angry. Was he just not going to talk to me? She wondered. He wasn't going to just not talk to her at all and sleep with her and leave. She wasn't going to have it.

'Are you going to at least talk to me?' she asked.

Spencer looked at her. 'What do you want me to say?'

Linda scoffed. 'Um, sorry, for starters. You embarrassed me in front of my friends.'

The car slowed, and Spencer diverted off the main highway down a bush track that she didn't recognise. 'Where are we going?' she asked.

'New spot,' he replied flatly.

The ute fell silent again as they bumped up and down the rough bush track. Darkness had fallen completely, and a kangaroo sat in the centre of the track up ahead, halting their progress. Spencer slowed the ute and gave a quick blip of the horn to scare it off the track. He continued down for another few minutes until they came into a clearing, and he wound down the windows and turned the ute off.

He turned to her. 'I'm sorry. I really am. I shouldn't have come at you like that. I didn't mean to embarrass you in front of your friends. I just love you so much, Linds. I don't want you to leave me.'

Linda breathed out, feeling the tension in the air leaving the ute. She placed her hand on Spencer's knee. 'Your too close to it, Spence. You can't see it. I love you. I'm not going anywhere.'

As the night progressed and Spencer had her laughing again, she got out of the ute and got into the back seat. Spencer took the hint and jumped in beside her as quick as he could. She kissed Spencer hungrily, and wanted to make him happy, to snap him out of this funk. She grabbed a condom from the centre console where Spencer kept them, unbuttoned her shorts and slid them down around her ankles, and then put her hand down the front of Spencer's shorts. He slowly pushed her back down onto the seat and lay down on top of her.

***

Spencer had stewed on it all night. Who was the fucking bitch to go around town with other men? Happily hugging them and talking with them for the whole town to see. It was an embarrassment to him, and an embarrassment to his family. His mother now hadn't spoken to him for a month, and he could see the toll it was beginning to take on his father. He hated her. He couldn't stand the sight of her. And knew she had to go away. For good.

As they made love, he boiled with rage. His whole body shook with it, and he looked down at her in the moonlight for one last time and made the decision as he slowly wrapped his hands around her neck. She tried to hit them away and then screamed out, 'Spencer! Stop! You're hurting me!' It was the last words she spoke. He watched her face as it turned red and he squeezed as hard as he could, harder than he ever had before, as tears streamed down his face. 'You did this! You did it! It's your fault!' He screamed at her as he felt her going limp and the life leaving her body.

Spencer got up off her and looked down. Her body lay back across the back seat with her shirt up and her shorts still around her feet. He was disgusted with her. And disgusted with himself. He felt himself shaking as the rage in his body turned to shock. What was he going to do? He needed to get rid of her body and make it look like it was something else.

Spencer opened the back passenger side door, grabbed her by the ankles, and dragged her out onto the dirt. She was heavier than he expected, and he struggled to get her moving again as he dragged her towards the ditch beside the road. He got her to the edge and took one last look at her body. It was a shame, really, but he knew she was pushing away from him and it was clear she didn't want to be with him anymore. It wouldn't be long before she had tried to get away, and he was yet to meet someone who had ever said no to him. She wouldn't be any different. He kicked her body forward, and it rolled three times, limp and flapping until she landed face first in the base of the ditch. He looked left and right, knowing no-one ever came down this way. It was between two neighbouring farms, and he knew it would take years before she was found.

Spencer turned to head back to his ute and had a brainwave. He un-tied his laces on one of his boots and slid down into the ditch to her body. He grabbed her hands and pulled them roughly behind her, and wrapped the laces around them, tying them as tightly as he could. He walked back up to the road and looked down again for the final time, and then got into his ute and drove off into the night.

His parents were away, so he knew no-one would have even noticed he was gone. He was meant to be babysitting his sister, Lisa, but she would have slept all the way through it, he was sure. It was 2:00am by the time he got home, and he parked his ute in his dad's spot in the garage and padded with one boot towards the door to the hallway. He jumped back in fright as he spied the outline of somebody standing in the doorway.

'Where have you been? I was worried.' Lisa asked.

'No-where, don't worry about it.'

Lisa pointed to his feet. 'Where's your other shoe?'

Spencer looked down. 'It's. In the car.' He looked back up at her and walked in close. 'Lisa, this never happened, ok? If you tell mum and dad, you're dead meat. I was here the whole night, alright?'

Chapter Twenty-Six

Nick sat in the interview room with Joanna and waited. It had been nearly an hour since they had got to Spencers and asked for him to come and visit them at the station, and he started to get worried. 'Where the hell is he?' he said into the empty space.

Joanna looked at her watch. 'It's been an hour.'

Constable Navarro knocked on their door and opened it. 'Spencer Hartford here to see you guys.'

Spencer stood behind her. 'Hey. Sorry I'm late.'

'Take a seat, Spencer,' he said.

Joanna had moved beside him and opened her notepad, and Spencer sat across from them, with his arms folded across his chest, in a classic defensive pose. 'So, what have you got for me?'

Nick decided to just lay it all out. The worst that could happen was that he would clamp up and say nothing. 'I've got a lot of things, Spencer. And not all of them are adding up.'

'Like?'

'Like your backyard. Your Oak tree.'

'What about it?'

'It's huge. And I spoke with the cop who found Emily. How did she manage to hang herself in the tree like that? She was metres up in the air. Where was the chair she stood on? The ladder? There was nothing.'

'Wait, wait, wait. What are you saying?'

'I think she was murdered Spencer.'

Spencer's mouth opened slowly, and a look of shock came across his face. His eyes were wide, and he put his face down into his hands. 'What. What are you telling me? Why would anybody want to murder her?'

It wasn't the reaction he expected. But successfully getting away with one murder was a sheer stroke of luck, in a different time. He wasn't going to go easy on him. 'Yes. I believe she was murdered. Her blood alcohol content was three times the limit, and she was drugged. Plus, her arms were covered in defensive wounds.'

Spencer sat quietly and watched him as he spoke. 'Well, who would do something like this? She had no enemies.'

Nick knew now was the time. 'I think you did it, Spencer.'

Spencer looked at them both in complete silence for what felt like thirty seconds, and then burst into a loud, hearty laughter. 'Are you being serious right now?'

'Deadly,' Joanna replied.

Spencer wiped tears from his eyes and slapped the desk. 'I thought you were meant to be the super detective? You've got this really, really wrong, Nick. Bec is going to kill you when I tell her this. Do you realise what you are saying?'

'I'm not bothered about Bec's reaction, Spencer. I just want the truth. Tell us what happened.'

Spencer folded his arms again and leaned back in the car. 'No, thank you. I don't think I will be speaking with you two again until a lawyer is present.'

Nick assumed that this was what would happen and hoped to glean more information out of him before he completely closed up. 'We have footage of you leaving the Adina Canberra at 7:00am and returning at 5:00am the night she died. Perfect amount of time to get to Edithvale, commit the crime and return.'

Spencer smiled. 'You think you've got it all figured out. I think you need to speak with Victoria, my assistant, before you go any further.'

'We will do that,' Joanna replied.

'Good. Because I'm sure she'll be happy to tell you that I spent the entire night with her.'

Nick hadn't prepared for that. He assumed she would have been at the Adina along with him. 'She didn't stay at the Adina?' he asked.

Spencer shook his head. 'You can speak to her for yourself. I'm not answering anything else. Will that be all?'

'Linda Mattazio,' Joanna said.

Nick watched as his mouth opened again, and he could see the tension in his body as he stiffened. 'Who told you about that?'

'We're police, Spencer. Your name is all over the case file,' he said with a smile. 'You didn't think we'd find out about it?'

'Lawyer,' Spencer said.

They tried a few more avenues of questioning, but all Spencer replied with were the words, 'Lawyer.' He left shortly after, and Joanna moved opposite to Nick again and sighed. 'What do you think?'

Nick rubbed his temples. 'Convenient alibi. We have to speak with Victoria. Get her side of the story.'

'I agree,' Joanna replied.

Joanna left Nick alone back at the station to go and get the footage Spencer had mentioned from the neighbours. She made her way toward the Eagleton property behind the Hartford's and when she got there; she parked out front of the enormous home, got out and admired it from the street. The property was a towering two storey concrete structure, with cedar timber battens affixed to the top floor of the building. It was ultra-modern and stuck out like a sore thumb in the street where every other home was a federation-style home. She wasn't sure what the Eagleton's did, but they must have had enough money to get around the strict heritage laws that were in place in the river town. Most buildings near the port were listed so that they couldn't be demolished. Whatever type of home this had been, it hadn't been so lucky.

She walked through the front gate and walked up the red clinker brick path and admired the neatly trimmed rose bushes. The front door opened as she reached the porch, and she eyed a similar camera setup to the one above the door that was on the front porch of the Hartford residence. A woman stood in the door dressed in neat moleskin pants and a white and blue striped, loose button-up shirt. She looked to be in her mid-50's but could've passed as someone much younger. She looked wealthy, and when she opened her mouth, sounded it too. 'Good morning, officer.'

'Good morning, I'm detective Joanna Gray with the Edithvale police. Hoping we could have a quick word?'

'Of course, come in.'

Joanna followed her into the cavernous entrance of the home and admired the artwork which adorned the walls. They were of all different types and varieties, and she stood at a giant painting of the Murray River and admired the artist's skills.

'That's the Murray River. Near Mildura,' the women said. She held out her hand. 'I'm Noelle Eagleton. Nice to meet you.'

'You too,' she replied. 'Did you paint these?'

Noelle laughed. 'Goodness, no. I wish. I'm an avid art collector.' She pointed towards her backyard. 'Is this about Emily? I can't believe it. I've been in Singapore for two weeks and only just heard the news when I got home. Absolutely terrible.'

'It is, I'm afraid. I was hoping if I could ask for some assistance on the matter?'

'Of course. Anything.'

Joanna walked near her back sliding door and looked out her window. She could see the back side of the Oak tree from where she stood. It loomed over the Eagleton's backyard like a spectre of death. She pointed out towards it. 'Do you have any cameras in your backyard?'

Noelle glanced out the back as well. 'I do. My husband was always a little nosy, bless his soul. Terrified of intruders, which was funny, we lived in Melbourne for most of our life. I told him Edithvale is much safer.' She began to walk towards the back hallway. 'Follow me.'

Joanna followed her down the hardwood floor lined hallway and admired the beautiful gardens at the rear of the property. There were giant Camellia's in full bloom which lined her back fence under the Oak tree, and she commented on their beauty. 'Your garden is beautiful. Camellias are my favourite flower,' she said.

Noelle reached a door and opened it into a small study. 'Thank you. They keep me busy. They bloom for a month or two and then make an almighty mess.' She pointed at a laptop sitting at the desk. 'This was my husbands. He passed last year. I don't know how to use it. I think the cameras run through that. Feel free to look through.'

Joanna sat down. She moved the mouse, and the screen came to life. She found the camera program and was happy to see them all online and functional. She clicked through each view until she stopped in her tracks. One of the views was from up high; and she guessed the camera must have been fixed on or near the roof of the house and had a perfect view into the Hartford's back yard. The screen caught the edge of the deck, and the rolling grass all the way down to the Oak tree. Joanna was frozen. If the footage went back far enough, the answers were right in front of her.

Joanna turned back to Noelle, who was looking at her phone. 'How far back does this footage go?'

Noelle looked at the laptop. 'Fred used to say a month. No idea, though.'

She snapped the screen shut. 'Do you mind if I take this?'

'Be my guest.'

Chapter Twenty-Seven

Emily stood deathly still as she looked at the gun in the man's hand. She held her hands up and could feel her whole-body convulsing in fear. 'Please don't hurt me.'

The man stepped over the threshold and closed the door quietly behind him. Remi ran up near them, and barked behind her, and he bent down and called the dog over. Remi cautiously walked over toward him, and he patted her gently on the head. 'Hello, little one,' he said as he scratched her under the chin.

'What do you want from me?' she said, as tears began to stream from her eyes.

The man stood slowly and kept the gun trained on Emily's centre mass. 'Walk,' he said. She turned and slowly walked down her hallway with Remi in tow. She looked at the images on her walls as she walked and remembered her life with Spencer. The first photo near the front door of their wedding, the happiest day of her life. She continued on to the middle years, when all of their friends were still young enough not to have kids, and the fun and adventures they had spent together. Next, the time when they were both fully fledged lawyers, and the tropical paradises and sprawling snow-capped mountain ranges that they had enjoyed together. The last truly fun times in their marriage. She slowed as she neared the end of the hallway and covered her mouth as she began to sob. What had she done? She looked at the photos of them, apart, with their friends now, both happy in the photos, in their own ways. Had she pushed him away? Was the breakdown of their marriage all her fault? She wondered if she would ever live to know.

Emily walked toward the kitchen and stood at the island bench next to the bottle of wine, and turned to look at the man. 'I'm guessing you're Miles?' she asked.

Miles smirked. 'You're a smart one.' He walked over to the bench top, and eyed the stack of pills and the wine bottle on the granite bench top and had an idea. If he shot her, the gunshot would easily be heard this time of night, and he didn't want to get too close to her. DNA these days was incredible. He knew that much through his job.

He slid the two packs of pills towards her, along with the wine bottle. 'Take them,' he said.

Emily looked down at the pills. 'What do you mean?'

'Take all of them. Or I'll shoot you right now. I know which way I'd rather go.'

He pulled out a bar stool on the island bench and rested his gun on the bench top in her direction. This had to work. He needed to get rid of her, and get rid of Bo's partner Amy, if he could find her. The bitch was proving much harder to find than he ever thought.

Emily slowly popped the Valium and Oxycodone pills out of their wrapper until there were roughly 40 pills sitting in front of her. They had been prescribed to her by her therapist months earlier, when she had suffered from a bout of depression, when her final round of IVF treatment with Spencer had failed. She looked down at the pills, and wondered whether these would be the things that would end her life. She moved to get her glass of wine from the cupboard and Miles jolted and grabbed the pistol quickly. 'Where are you fuckin' going?'

Emily held her hands up. 'Getting a glass.'

Miles placed the gun back down and gave her a curt nod.
He watched as she reached up high in the top cupboard and
grabbed a fresh glass. She was thin, and had a great figure,
and he was annoyed he had to try and leave no evidence. She
could've been abit of fun. He watched as she slowly tipped
the pills into her mouth one by one and took big gulps of her
red wine. At one point, she gagged and nearly vomited, but
held her nerve and kept going. He almost admired her. Most
of them screamed and begged. She did none of the sort, just
quietly met her maker.

Emily pulled the end stool out at the other end of the
island bench and sat down when she had finished. She looked
slightly woozy on her feet, but he felt like it hadn't really
kicked in yet. She still seemed lucid. 'Why?' she asked him.

Miles had thought about it himself on the drive down from
Griffith. He had no choice. His undercover role with the last
of the Italian crime families in Griffith had been one that had
scared the shit out of him when he had first been embedded.
But slowly, over a few years, they made him a part of the
family, and he had struggled to extract any meaningful
information out to his contacts in the force without feeling a
deep sense of shame. When he was blooded into the family a
year earlier, he had made the choice to go all in. He would
keep feeding the police false information, but would enjoy the

life and perks that the family had bestowed upon him. He had started as a courier and a cook, and then had moved to their hired muscle, but it wasn't until he had killed his first man, under the boss's orders, that he knew he could never go back. He had to get rid of these two women quickly, as they were the only two people in the world now that knew his secret.

'Because I have no choice,' he replied finally.

They sat in silence again, and as the minutes ticked over; he sat and watched the woman. She still sat rock solid in her seat, drinking her wine and looking straight ahead into the kitchen. That amount of drugs should've knocked her out in minutes he would've thought. And he cautiously eyed his watch, wary of the amount of time he had spent in the house.

Miles held the empty packet of Valium up in her direction. 'What are these for, anyway?

Emily sighed. 'Doctors said I had depression.'

Miles watched the little dog come in from outside through the dog door, and he looked out the back windows into the yard. He stood up and walked to the back doors and eyed the pool and gardens, and the giant Oak tree at the rear of the backyard. He looked at the ominous shape in the night and a light bulb went off in his head. 'Where is your garage?' he asked.

'Next to the front door,' Emily replied. 'Why?'

'You'll see.' He held the gun up at her again. 'Go.'

Emily stood and stumbled slightly on her feet, but then remained steady. He held the gun on her. He didn't have any more patience. 'Walk.' She walked on towards the garage door, and he watched the small dog walking beside her. She slowed as she reached the door and went for the handle, opening the door inward and turning on the light.

'Stay here,' he said.

Miles walked into the garage and let his eyes acclimatise to the bright fluorescent lighting. He walked near a timber work bench and soon found what he was after, a thick length of rope. He remembered one of the bosses talking about an accountant back in the day who had wronged him, and how he had strung him up in the tree out front of his house and left him for dead. He had told him it was the easiest murder he had ever done. No-one expected a thing.

Miles held the rope in one hand and the gun in the other. 'Backyard,' he said.

Emily walked through her home for the final time with Remi by her side as Miles followed. She slid open the back door and stood on her back deck, where she had entertained her friends. She admired her pool and remembered late night swims with Spencer, and looked out across her beautiful garden and the giant Oak tree in the centre of it at the back. She could feel the drugs taking effect, and felt light on her feet. She did not know what his plans were for her now. Maybe he was going to tie her up and leave her for dead? She had no idea. But as he gestured her to walk forward onto the grass, she didn't care anymore. She had no fight left. The drugs had taken that away from her.

Miles walked slowly behind her and eyed the giant Oak tree in the distance. He knew how to tie a noose from his days back in the scouts and held his pistol under his arm pit while he quickly fashioned the knot. Emily slowed as she got closer to the Oak tree and stopped.

As she went to turn around, with her senses inhibited, she didn't have time to react as Miles jumped forward with a violent force and wrapped the noose tightly around her neck. She spun and tried to paw at his arms and fight as hard as she could, and with her last ounce of strength, she scrapped and clawed at him valiantly and screamed as she felt his nails dig into her forearms. He pushed her backwards hard, and her head hit the earth before her back, knocking her into a half unconsciousness. Now she was temporarily disabled, Miles grabbed her hand and slid her under the Oak, all while

Remi growled and barked at him. 'Shut up!' he yelled at the little dog, who yelped and ran back up towards the deck.

Miles threw the long end of the rope up over the branch and wrapped the rope around his hands twice for a better grip. He thought it may have been harder, but by looking at her thin frame, he assumed she weighed half his weight, as he easily lifted her limp body up in the tree. He tied the long end around the lowest branch and stood back to admire his bright idea.

Emily was jolted back into consciousness and felt the noose tight around her neck. She eyed Miles standing on the grass, looking up at her with satisfaction, and she thrashed and writhed, fighting for her life. As she felt the last of her breath leaving her lungs, the last thing she saw was Remi, who stood in the centre of the lawn, helplessly watching her as she slipped away.

Chapter Twenty-Eight

As Nick waited to see how Joanna went with finding any more footage from the neighbouring homes, he decided to head back to the motel room to try and speak with Bec and clear the air after their argument at the pub. He knew he was just trying to follow the evidence, trying to do his job. He was sure she would have calmed down by now; she needed to understand.

Nick reached the room and swiped the keycard in the door and walked inside. The cleaners had been through, and the room looked immaculate. He walked to the cupboard and slid open the door. Only his suitcase remained. The various tops Bec had had hanging up were no longer there, and he walked into the bathroom to see no toiletries or makeup of hers left.

Nick tried her phone again and waited to see if she would answer this time. 'Hello,' she said.

'I'm at the room. Where are you?'

'Room 17,' she replied, hanging up the phone.

That didn't sound good, he thought. He splashed his face with some water and ran his hands through his hair and headed for the door. As he walked to her room, he struggled to remember the last time they had had a decent fight. Most of the arguments he had with previous partners were always work related, but Bec was different. She understood. She knew how hard his job was. She knew the pressure he was under at all times. Their fights were always over more meaningless things. Who would pay for dinner? Why did you put the colours in with the whites in the wash? Never anything major. This was serious.

Nick knocked gently on the door and heard Bec speak from inside. 'Come in.'

Bec sat on the end of her bed in her workout gear, and he could see she had been crying. He felt terrible. He just wanted to hug her in that moment, but he knew he had to explain himself first. He pulled out the chair at the table near the door and sat down. 'You changed rooms.'

'I did. I've been speaking with Spencer.'

'And?'

She looked at him as her face turned red and yelled, 'And?! And I told you to drop it, Nick! You brought him in for questioning?! What the hell are you doing?! His wife is dead, Nick! My best friend is dead! Not everything is a case for you!'

'Bec, please, we have..'

She held her hand up. 'I don't want to hear it. I don't care what you think you have. Spencer did not do it. I repeat, he did not do it, Nick. I trust him. He wouldn't lie to me!'

'You're not listening to me, Bec.'

She stood up, with tears streaming down her face. 'You need to make a choice. Right here, right now. You either drop this whole business with Spencer, or we are done.'

Nick sat still in the chair. How could she be so wrong? He just wanted to shake her. She was smart. Smarter than most, but she was too close to it. He wanted her to see the evidence. But now was not the time. He wasn't going to drop it. He was going to get answers and then present her with the facts. She would change her mind when she saw it.

'I'm not having this conversation,' he said.

Bec wiped tears from her eyes. 'I love you, Nick. But it sounds like you've made your decision. Please, just get out.'

Nick walked outside the room and stood out in the sunshine in the carpark. Everything was silent, and he could hear the blood rushing through his ears. He wasn't going to lose Bec over this. He would never give up. He would get answers and prove her wrong.

His phone rang, and he pulled it from his pocket. 'Hello?'

'Nick, It's Joanna. I've got the footage from the house behind. Meet me at the station in ten.'

Nick walked straight from Bec's room and got straight back in his car. Joanna's car was parked out front of the police station when he got there, and he got out and quickly made his way inside. Up in their makeshift office, Joanna had her laptop plugged into a larger computer monitor. He sat down beside her, rubbed his eyes, and felt the familiar tingle on the end of his tongue. He needed a drink.

Joanna looked at him warily. 'Are you ok? You look terrible.'

Nick nodded. 'I'm fine.'

She pointed at the screen. 'You ready?'

'Let's do this.'

An unknown number came up on his mobile phone screen, and he answered it. 'Hello?'

'Nick it's Prue Thornton here. Long time. How are you?'

Nick groaned internally. Prue Thornton was firstly a friend, but secondly a journalist. If she was calling, the news was already out. 'I'm good, Prue. I'm guessing this isn't a social call?'

'No. I've gotten word you've arrested Spencer Hartford, the liberal MP? Is this about his wife's death?'

'We have. Look, I can't tell you much right now. But when we get a little closer, you will be the first to know, alright?'

'Thanks Nick. You're the best.'

'I know.'

Nick hung up the phone. 'Reporters. Already.'

'God, news travels fast,' Joanna said.

'We need to move quickly. Let's see what we have here,' he replied.

Joanna slowly fast forwarded through the days leading up to Emily's death and stopped at vision of Victoria and Spencer swimming in his pool.

'This is good quality footage,' he said as he watched them kissing in the centre of the pool. 'Far out. He's got no shame, does he?'

Joanna sighed. 'Some men think they can get away with anything. I think we're going to see everything here.'

'Agreed.'

Joanna fast forwarded the footage up to the day of Emily's death and pressed stop at 3:30pm in the afternoon. They watched as her dog, Remi, happily ran around the back lawn and dug a hole in the garden near the Oak tree. Joanna pressed times two forward, and they watched as the sun slowly began to set. There was nothing on the screen until Nick eyed a shape coming out of the back door. 'Stop.' He pointed at the shape. 'I think that's her.'

Joanna stopped the footage, and they both sat deathly still. As the scene played out, both of their mouths slowly opened in unison. Emily Hartford, woozy on her feet, walked slowly out of her door, across her deck and onto her grass. Behind her, a man in black held a pistol in his hand, and a rope in the other. As she reached the Oak tree, a struggle ensued, and they watched as Emily fought valiantly for her life. She scratched and kicked her attacked until he pushed her hard backwards, and the back of her head hit the grass with a hard thud. After it, it looked like she was knocked out.

The next bit was the most distressing. He tightened the noose around her neck, threw the rope over the top branch, and slowly pulled the rope until she was hanging high in the tree. He fastened the end of the rope around the lowest branch, which was higher up than Nick could reach, and walked back towards the house, and slowly turned to watch her final moments. There was something about the walk, the way he stood, that stopped Nick in his tracks. He watched Emily as she thrashed and writhed, and slowly faded, until, with one final twitch, she was dead.

Nick looked across at Joanna, who was had tears in her eyes, with her hands over her mouth. 'Oh, my god.'

Nick pointed to the man on the screen. 'Can you zoom in?'

Joanna didn't reply, but he watched as her hand shook before it landed on the mouse. She clicked to the menu, took a screenshot and then zoomed in on the man's face. He was amazed at the quality of cameras these days as he looked at a high-definition image of a man he had worked with in Sydney in his early days on the force.

'Jesus Christ. That's Miles Cook,' he said.

Chapter Twenty-Nine

Chief Inspector Mark Johnson sat at his desk in his office in the Sydney homicide headquarters and heard his phone ring on the table. It had been quite a long day, and his mind was already at dinner with his wife for her birthday that he had planned a few weeks ago. It was a seafood restaurant that they had been trying to get into for months, and he knew she would be thrilled with the fine dining experience.

Mark answered his phone on the third ring. 'Hello?'

'Hi Mark. Katherine in media relations. How are you?'

Mark groaned internally. A call from Katherine was never good. 'Afternoon Kath, what have one of my guys done now?'

Katherine laughed. 'Not every call is bad news, you know.'

'You're right there. Happy to not be the boss of the bloke that tasered that little old lady the other month.'

Her tone turned sombre. 'No. That was not a fun week.'

'So, what can I do for you?'

'We are getting reports from local media down in Edithvale that federal MP Spencer Hartford has been arrested. Under the suspicion of murdering his wife?'

News travels fast, he thought. His phone call with Nick was only a few hours ago. 'That is correct.'

'Far out. A little heads up would've been nice.'

Mark knew the media department better than most, and knew that although they touted there that all secrets were safe with them, he knew of more than one leak that had been let out behind closed doors. Even his own departments hadn't been safe over the last few years.

'Sorry. I should've let you know. All top secret, hush hush, you know how it is.'

'Yes, I do. Would you like me to start putting together a media release?'

'I'll email you through details shortly. Don't want to put anything out too early.'

'No worries, have a good day.'

'Bye.'

He leaned back in his chair, and fist pumped the air. One of the sergeants at the desk outside his office looked up expectantly, and he quickly brought his excitement level down a peg. If the media had heard about it, that was good news. Nick must have cracked him, must have made the arrest. If he couldn't take him down for Linda all those years ago. He'd get him now for Emily.

His phone rang again on the desk, and he grabbed at the receiver. 'Hello?'

'Is this Chief Inspector Mark Johnson?'

'Speaking?'

'Hi Chief, this is Gabby Hodges, at the N.S.W Forensic Biology and DNA Analysis laboratory. How are you today?'

'I'm well, Gabby. What can I do for you today?'

'I have been trying to contact Detective Sergeant Nick Vada about a DNA requested submitted by you last week. I have you down as a secondary contact.'

Mark leaned forward in his chair. He squeezed the phone tighter than usual and felt time slow down. There weren't many cases he had as a detective that had gotten away from him, but this one had, and it was the image in back of his mind, seeing Linda's body lying in the ditch that never left him, along with young Spencer Hartford's smug, smiling face in the interview room.

'He must be busy. Do you have any results?'

'I do. I'm happy to say it's a match. The DNA sample you provided was found on the shorts and on the top. There was also a tiny blood sample with the evidence that you submitted, which we were able to get this time around as well. I checked that too, another match.'

***

Nick sat at the desk dead still. He watched the video over twice in complete silence. Joanna watched him intently, and desperately wanted to know who he was talking about. After watching it through a third time, he leaned back in his chair and put his hands over his face. 'Fuck,' was all he said.

'What is it? Who the hell is Miles Cook?'

'He was a senior constable when I knew him. Last I heard, he had transferred to the drug squad.'

'Well, what the hell is he doing in Edithvale?!'

'I don't know. Fuck. I don't know.' He pressed his forehead down on the edge of the table and closed his eyes, trying to clear his head.

'What the hell are we going to do about Spencer?' Joanna asked.

Nick sat back up. 'There's nothing to do. He didn't do it.'

'What about Bec?'

'I don't know.'

His phone buzzed on the bench. He reached across and picked it up and looked at the screen. Seeing it was the chief, he answered immediately. 'Hey Chief.'

The chief was laughing. 'I have news.'

Nick placed the phone on speaker and put it on the bench. 'I've got you on speaker here with Joanna as well. Hopefully, good news please. We need it.'

'Well, the good news is you bloody got Spencer Hartford! I had Katherine in media calling me, the news is already going around. Great work.'

'It wasn't him, chief. We got the wrong person.'

'Wait, what? What do you mean?'

'You ever heard of a cop named Miles Cook?'

'No. Doesn't ring a bell. Why?'

'He killed Emily Hartford. We have camera footage from the neighbours' security camera. The bastard strung her up in the tree at gunpoint.'

'Jesus Christ. And you're saying he's a copper?'

'Was, I guess. I knew him ten years ago. I'm guessing he's a crook now. I'll email you the footage. Chief, we've fucked up big time. Spencer will sue us for this.'

The chief was thrown, but managed to maintain his smile. This was merely a speed hump. He still had gotten what he was always after. 'Well, it doesn't matter, because I have more news.'

'Go on,' Joanna replied.

'We got him for Linda Mattazio. The DNA you submitted was a match.'

Nick sat in silence and tried to re-assemble his thoughts. He knew he had Spencer right where he wanted him for Emily, and the chances of them solving the Mattazio murder were next to none. Now it had all been flipped on its head.

'You guys there?' the chief asked.

Nick cleared his throat. 'Yeah. Sorry. Shit. I didn't expect that. I didn't expect that at all. What do you want to do?'

'I want you to arrest the bastard. I'll have an arrest warrant for him within the next five minutes.'

'What about Miles Cook?' he asked.

'Let me search the database. I'll look up his history, see what he's been up to.'

Joanna was furiously typing as they spoke. She spun the laptop screen in Nick's direction with a photo of Miles' face, sans-beard, with an active sign against his profile in the N.S.W officers' database.

'He's still a cop. Joanna's got his profile here.'

'Good. That makes it easier for us. Let me make a few calls.'

There was another knock at the door, and Sarah Navarro popped her head in again. 'Sorry to bother you, detectives. We have an Amy Davidson here. Says she has some information for you?'

Nick turned to Sarah. 'Sure, bring her up.'

Chapter Thirty

Spencer walked out of the station into the hot sunshine and felt his skin crawling. His back was damp with sweat, and he moved to his car slowly, trying to act as normal as possible. He got inside and pressed the ignition and sat in silence, trying to figure out his next move.

He hadn't killed Emily. And he couldn't believe that Nick Vada would think that he did. He had always loved her, more than anything in this world, but their relationship had been dead. Her suspicions about an affair before she passed, sadly, had been true. He had started a relationship with Victoria within the first week she became his assistant. She was young, smart, beautiful, and was bursting with an energy that excited him. She reminded him of Emily when they first met at work, still full of youthful vigour, with a daring sense of adventure.

Time had worn that dare and vigour from Emily, and after their third IVF attempt had failed, he felt like she had closed off from him completely, being unable to come to grips with the fact that they may never be parents. This was right around the time his political career was seemingly shooting to the stratosphere, with every new gushing article in the news better than the last. He knew he was still very young to be rising this fast within the ranks of his party, but he could picture a future in his head where he could make it all the way and potentially even make the top job.

He had tried his best to bring Emily along with him at first. He had brought her along to events, to meet and greets, and to private dinners as he tried his best to network and gain new relationships with people higher up in life than either of them had been before. But Emily was gone. The bubbly and bright woman from the start of their marriage was done. She would sit, dead eyed with a fake smile, and not make any conversations with any of the other wives in the room. It was getting so bad at one point he told her she needed to go see a therapist, which she did. The therapist diagnosed her with depression after her third failed IVF treatment, and he hoped with the right pills, the old Emily might return.

He had been wrong however, and her jealousy and sniping at him come to a head when she first accused him of cheating on her with his first assistant, Jessica. The thought had been so ludicrous, so out of this world that he couldn't believe it at the time, and he disregarded it entirely. It wasn't until he met Victoria that he knew she was different. She was the bright, vivacious, highly social partner that he needed in this life to take him to the top. It also helped that she was the most beautiful woman in the room, and she seemed madly in love with him. Their love had been almost immediate from their first meeting, and he had promised her that one day he would divorce Emily and she would become his wife.

Emily dying was completely out of this world to him, and his mind and body were still filled with grief, so much so that he felt sick about it. It was clear to him that she had committed suicide, unable to face the fact that he was going to leave her for Victoria, and went out in one last final act of defiance. He still couldn't believe it as he sat in his car that she was gone.

But the biggest thing that had him in shock was Nick Vada mentioning the name Linda Mattazio. It was like hearing a name from a different dimension, from a different time in his life. He had suppressed the memories so far down, so deep, that he never ever thought they would come back up again. The last time he had heard that name took him back in his mind to a few years earlier, back when he had got his first seat with the party. Two of the top ministers took him out to a men's club in Canberra and sat him down for a private discussion. They knew all about the Mattazio case, all of the dirty details, and asked him what he knew about it all. He sat in that dark, cigar smoke filled room with apprehension and lied through his teeth. He wasn't going to let a mistake he made in his past ruin his future. He was better than that. They promised him they had contacts in the police who could suppress it, make it disappear, and ensure it would never see the light of day again. How wrong they were.

Spencer accelerated out of the car park and headed for the Quest motel in town. He had told Victoria that she could stay at his house, but she had warned him against it; she knew how it would look, the optics. It was that type of thinking that he needed at this time, smart thinking.

His phone rang, and he answered it without looking at the screen. 'Hello.'

'Spencer, it's Bec.'

'Bec. How are you?'

'I should be asking you. It's all over the news. What did Nick do?'

'He arrested me, Bec! He dragged me into an interview room and accused me of killing Emily!' Spencer knew he had to be wary of the detective, but considering he had seemed to know a lot more than what he had originally thought about his past, he thought he may as well throw a spanner in his private life. It may slow him down abit. 'He threatened me, Bec.' He waited for a beat, and sniffled, like he was crying. 'He grabbed me by the collar and told me I was going to jail for the rest of my life.'

Spencer could hear how upset Bec was. 'I'm so sorry, Spencer. I told him you didn't do it. I know you. I know you would never.'

Spencer was smiling now; he had her right where he wanted her. 'Well, can you speak to him about it? He's gone right behind your back, Bec.'

'I can try. Thank you for letting me know. I don't know what else to say.'

He pulled into the car park of the motel and went to the far end room to park in beside Victoria's red coupe. 'I have to go, Bec.'

'Goodbye Spence.'

Spencer pressed the end button on the call and couldn't wipe the smile off his face. Fuck the prick. Maybe Bec would leave him. The bastard deserved it. He would never get him. He opened his iPhone and clicked on his news app. His eyes widened as he read the top headline. 'BREAKING - Federal MP arrested over murder of wife.'

'Fuck!' He punched his steering wheel as hard as he could. 'Fuck! Fuck! Fuck!'

Spencer threw his phone into his cup holder and got out of his car, slamming the door in the process. He walked up to Victoria's room and knocked on the door. He heard footsteps, and she stood in the opening, smiling in his direction. She was the one face that he needed to see. 'Hi,' he said.

'Well. You're quite popular right now,' she said with a chuckle. She opened the door and walked over to the dining table where her laptop and iPad were both sitting. The TV was also on, on Channel Four news, and he read the breaking news tape at the bottom of the screen. 'I'm going to need a favour,' he said, sitting on the end of the bed.

Victoria stood up, walked over to him, and stood between his legs. She wrapped her arms around his head and held him tightly. 'You know I would do anything for you, babe.'

Spencer looked up. 'I need you to tell them about our last night in Canberra.'

'In any other circumstances, I'd say it was the perfect night.'

He thought back to the night, and the hot spa that was on the roof of Victoria's apartment building. He had played it through his mind more than any other night in his life, except one, and felt deep guilt and shame. Yes, he might have been having fun. But his wife's life had ended. And he wasn't there to stop it. He might be cold-hearted and, at times callous, but he had a conscience. Or so he thought.

'Do you want me to go to the police station right now?' Victoria asked. 'We need to get on top of this.'

Spencer watched the TV screen that was just beside her and watched the news unfolding before him. His face was plastered on the screen, and it soon changed to the footage from his Instagram profile of him smiling and placing his hand on the small of Victoria's back, looking like a royal couple. It looked really bad. 'Yes, we do. I'm going to stay here if that's ok? I wouldn't be shocked if the media are already on their way to the house.'

Chapter Thirty-One

Mark hung the phone up from Nick, still with a smile on his face. The chance to close a twenty-year-old mystery was a rare one, and he was proud of his protégé. Sometimes things were simple, and sometimes they weren't, and as he typed Miles Cook into his laptop, he thought that this second issue might be the latter.

The profile opened, and he looked at the man staring back at him through the screen. He looked young, around mid to late 30s, and had a close-cropped hair cut and dark brown eyes. He read through his history on the job, and could almost tell his story before he read it. Young up and comer, ready to make sergeant in his early 30s, no wife, no kids, transfers to narcotics, and as he clicked into his history in narcotics, the files went blank. It screamed undercover. It was the only answer. He looked up his last commanding officer in the narcotics division and read the name. Peter Winter. He smiled at the screen. This one might be easier than he thought.

Mark pulled out his mobile phone and dialled Peter's number from his contacts. He had worked alongside him many years earlier as a detective and had known him well back then. He had played a few rounds of golf with him over the years as well. Peter wouldn't bullshit him.

Peter answered on the second ring. 'G'day mate. Long time.'

'Pete, mate, how are you? How's Julie and the kids?'

'Good, they're all good. Only one left at home these days, gonna' be a sad day when she's out.'

'I know the feeling,' Mark said with a chuckle. Of his two children, only his daughter still remained at home, while she finished her university degree.

'What can I do you for?' Peter asked.

'Miles Cook,' Mark said.

Peter all of a sudden sounded deadly serious. 'Where did you hear that name?'

'Do you want me to say over the phone?'

There was silence for a beat. 'No. You at head office?'

'I am. Still on the fifth.'

'Meet me down at the café in ten?'

'Will do.'

Down at the café, Mark walked through the entrance and looked out across the room. It was late afternoon, and the tables were sparsely occupied, mostly by people with laptops alone looking for some privacy. Peter sat in the far corner of the shop next to a high row of indoor fern pop plants. He waved him over.

Mark walked up and shook his hand. 'Sorry for all the cloak and dagger,' Peter said.

Mark sat down. 'So, I'm guessing you have heard of Miles Cook? You're the last listed commanding officer for him.'

'I was. I am. I'm still his boss.'

'So, what's he doing? I'm assuming he's undercover?'

Peter looked at him with suspicion. 'What's this all about, anyway? What's got you so interested in him?'

Mark held his phone out in Peter's direction with the Sydney Herald newspaper website open. 'You seen all this business with Spencer Hartford? The Liberal MP who killed his wife?'

Peter looked at the screen. 'Yeah, I did. Heard you had Nick Vada up there on it.'

'The woman who died is his girlfriend's best friend.'

'Shit. Well, I feel sorry for that MP then. He won't be getting out of anything with Vada on it.'

'Therein lies the issue. He didn't do it.'

Peter sipped from his coffee. 'Isn't that what they all say?'

'Miles Cook did it.'

Peter's cup clattered on the saucer, and he leaned forward. 'What?! What do you mean?'

'Detective Vada has crystal clear footage of him stringing the young woman, Emily Hartford, up in a tree in her back garden. Was initially written off as a suicide.'

Peter's mouth opened, and Mark could see he was clearly in shock. He clearly was still an active officer, and obviously very deeply entrenched undercover still. 'How does he know it's him? And how the hell did Vada work all of this out?'

'Apparently, he worked with him for a short time, years ago. I'll have this footage in my inbox momentarily.' He sipped from his coffee and grimaced at the burnt beans.

'Jesus, this café is still terrible. Coffee's shit. So, are you going to tell me what Cook is involved in?'

Peter slouched back in the booth and rubbed his face. Mark had never seen him this shaken up before. This was clearly something big. 'Miles was in the drug squad for a couple of years. Real rising star. We singled him out in his fourth year in the squad. No wife, no kids, and spoke Italian. He's second generation.'

'Italian?'

Peter grinned. 'The Calabrian mafia. Everyone has moved on with the designer shit. The Vietnamese and Chinese are pushing it all through the city these days, but the Italians still have a stranglehold on the weed market. And until it's legalised, it's still a multi-million-dollar business.'

'I thought they were long gone? I didn't even know any mafia in Australia still existed?'

'It does. And they've somehow managed to get into illegal vape production. It's doubled their output. Massive business. They're making money hand over fist.'

'So, Miles is in with them?'

Peter nodded. 'He was. He is, I guess. He started hanging round with a low-level drug dealer a few years back, and has now worked his way to near the top.'

Mark's phone buzzed with an email from Nick. He showed the screen to Peter, and he read it. 'Open it. I need to see it.'

Mark opened the email and clicked on the video link. He looked over both shoulders to ensure there were no peeping eyes around and turned the phone to landscape mode. Both of the senior officers, the best at what they did for a time, leaned in together and watched the camera footage, which was much clearer than their time when they were detectives together.

They watched as Emily marched forward, woozy on her feet, preparing mentally for her untimely demise. They watched the dark figure behind her with a pistol at the ready, hand steady, with the full confidence of a man who was trained to protect the public from the very person he had become. They watched the struggle ensue, the final fight for her life, and then the noose. The noose around her neck, him pulling the rope tight and lifting her up; him tying it off and standing back in satisfaction at what he had just done. In that moment, the light from the deck hit his face perfect, and illuminated it for all to see.

'Fuck. I can't believe it. You're right. That's Miles,' Peter said.

'He's got to go down for this, Peter.'

Peter looked down at the screen and shook his head. 'Fuck. I know. We were so close. He had them over a barrel. This is going to set us back years.'

'We can't have our officers, no matter how undercover they are out killing members of the public.'

'I know.'

'Do you know how we can get on to him?'

Peter opened his phone. 'Let me call his contact, see if we can get him out of hiding. He needs to go down for this.'

Chapter Thirty-Two

A young woman walked through the door of the interview room with a toddler in tow, and Joanna looked at Nick with raised eyebrows. She nervously looked behind the door quickly as she entered in the room and then passed her phone over to the toddler and sat him on the chair next to the wall.

She introduced herself. 'Hi. My name's Amy Davidson.'

'Hi Amy, I'm Detective Sergeant Nick Vada.' He pointed over to Joanna. 'And this is Detective Joanna Gray.'

'Hi,' she said with a meek wave. 'I have information you need to hear. I think I know who killed Emily Hartford.'

Nick placed his iPhone on the table. 'Do you mind if I record this?' Amy nodded. 'And who do you think killed Emily Hartford?'

Amy frowned. 'Miles Cook. He's an undercover cop. I think.'

Nick leaned forward in his chair. 'Tell us everything you know.'

Amy pulled a tissue out of her handbag and wiped her nose. 'My partner, Bo, was tied up with some bad people up in Griffith. Really bad people. Anyway, he owed these people money, a lot of money. He had unpaid debts.'

'And let me guess, he started working for them to repay those debts?'

'Correct. And that's where he met Miles. Or 'Squirrel', as they called him up there. He was a cook when they met. Then they ran drugs from Griffith all the way to Perth. They got really close.' She wiped a tear from her eyes. 'They were the good times.'

'And then?'

'And then one day, he came to Bo in private and laid it all out. He was undercover with the N.S.W police force in the narcotics division. He had gotten close to Bo and didn't want to see him go down for all of the shit they were doing. He wanted to save him. He wanted to do a deal.'

'So how did Emily get involved?' Joanna asked.

'Bo was conflicted. He didn't know who to turn to. He didn't know whether the deal was legit, and it wasn't like he could go to another cop and ask. I'm from Edithvale, and I'd seen Emily Hartford's face in the paper. It said she was a trusted lawyer. I thought I would go to her and ask her if it all was legitimate.'

Ned the toddler dropped the phone down on the ground and Amy swept down and picked it up. Her face was red now, and tears streaked her makeup. 'And then. I hadn't heard from Bo in a few days, and I was worried. I drove up to Griffith to try and find him and finally got a hold of him when I got to town. Miles was with him and wanted to finalise the deal. He took us out into the bush.' She stopped and wiped her tears again, trying her best to maintain the last bits of her makeup. 'And he shot Bo. He killed him.'

Nick looked at the women in front of him in shock and felt an anger towards her that he knew he had to hide. This whole debacle had started with her and her partner and had ended an innocent life for no reason. Emily was simply in the wrong place at the wrong time and had managed to inadvertently get involved in some serious business, which was none of her doing. He could see it all play out in front of him, like pieces on a chess board. Miles rising within the ruthless organisation, getting deeper and deeper and beginning to blur the lines between right and wrong. It was obvious to him that by the time he had offered the deal that he had probably already made the ultimate decision. He had decided to turn against what was right, and go against his role undercover, and truly turn against his own for greed.

Nick gritted his teeth and asked, 'What happened next?'

'I was in the car. It was so dark, there were people speaking and then Miles just lifted the gun and Bo dropped.' Her chest heaved up and down as she tried to control herself. 'I was so scared. I slipped out of the back door and ran into the bush. I was so scared they would find me. I ended up being near a main highway and I hitched a ride to the nearest town, and then got a ride back to Edithvale.'

'Where was Ned?' Joanna asked.

Amy rustled his hair, and the young boy looked at the two policemen. Nick thought he was lucky to even still have his mother on this earth with how close she came to death. 'He was with my parents,' she replied.

'So, did you see Emily again after the first meeting?' Joanna asked.

'I did. I got back into town and went to her straight away. I knew what gym she went to. Caught her in the carpark. Told her everything.'

Nick shook his head. He couldn't hold it in any longer. 'You could've led Cook straight to her.'

Amy looked at him. 'I know.' Her tears got even worse. 'I know. I'm sorry. I wish I could take it all back. I'm so sorry.'

'Why didn't you just go straight to the police?' he asked.

'Because when I was hiding in the bushland, Miles said if I said anything, he would tell the police I murdered Bo. And Ned would lose his mother, too.'

Nick looked at her blankly. 'With no evidence or DNA, he couldn't have done a thing.'

'Well, how would I know that? He's a cop and I'm not. He can do anything.'

Nick held himself back. He couldn't be too critical of her. She didn't know the ins and outs of a murder investigation, and seeing her partner being killed in cold blood would've been traumatic.

'That politician didn't kill Emily, I'm sure of it. It was Miles.' She held her phone out. 'He's been messaging me from an unknown number. Says he's going to get me like he did Emily if I say anything to anyone. I need protection.'

'We can protect you,' he said. 'But you need to get Miles out in the open for us. We need to arrest him.'

Amy looked down at her phone. 'Whatever I can to do to help. I just want him gone for good.'

Nick led Amy down to Greg Baseley's office with Joanna and sat Amy down with the inspector and got her to tell him everything again. Greg sat and listened intently, writing the odd note down on the pad in front of him as she spoke. The story as it came out the second time was flat and with less emotion, like that first time had been the massive emotional release that Amy had needed. When she finished, Joanna led her and her son out to a small tearoom and Nick sat across from the old inspector as he shook his head.

'Gee, you've stuffed this up big time,' Greg said. 'Hartford's face is all over the TV. It'll be in the newspapers tomorrow.'

Nick opened the video on his phone and slid it over the desk. Greg picked it up and sat in silence as the footage ran, and he watched his expression of mild curiosity turn to shock during the 1 minute 15 second video.

'Jesus Christ.' He slid the phone back over the desk. 'And he's a copper?'

Nick nodded. 'Undercover. Drug squad.'

Greg sighed. 'Well, not for long. This used to happen all the time. Money does crazy things to a person. How's Bec holding up?'

Nick placed both of his hands on top of his head. 'That problem is near the bottom of the list right now.'

'Shouldn't think like that. She should be up top. She's a good woman, that one.'

'I know. And she's not happy that I brought in Spencer for questioning. But it's about to get a whole lot worse.'

'Why's that?'

'Because we got a DNA match on him for the Mattazio murder. Matched his DNA to blood on the victim's clothing. Chief is getting an arrest warrant for us as we speak.'

'Jesus. You lot have been busy. He'll be a happy man. That was the one that got away from him for a long time. I remember someone chasing up an old lead on that out this way a few years back. Is there anything I can do to help? It's going to be a big deal around here.'

'Just keep a cell empty. You'll have a new guest tonight,' Nick said with a grin.

Chapter Thirty-Three

Nick and Joanna left Amy at the station, and Greg Baseley promised she would be in safe hands until Miles Cook was in custody. Joanna knew of two sexual and domestic assault victims' safe houses in Edithvale and told Nick he guessed they'd be taken there for the time being.

Nick sat in his car across from the police station and dialled Bec for the third time today. He text her as well and could see that she had read the message, but he was yet to receive a reply. He wished she would answer. He wanted to tell her everything. He needed her to know the truth, and he needed her calm mind more than ever in the craziness that was surrounding him. His body ached for a drink, like it did anytime he was stressed, and he wondered whether Joanna would notice if he stopped near a bottle shop and ran in for a small bottle of something to take the edge off.

Joanna got into the car and looked at him. 'Are you ok? You look like shit.'

Nick looked straight ahead. 'Yeah. A lot going on today.'

'Tell me about it. Trouble seems to follow you,' she said with a laugh.

His phone rang, and he looked at the screen in his car, hopeful it was Bec who was calling. It was a private number, and he answered, 'Hello?'

'Nick, Hattie.'

Nick was disappointed. 'Hey Hattie, sorry I didn't have your number saved.'

'No bother. Look, I did some digging, and may have done a little bit of illegal hacking into government phone records, but I managed to get all of the phone tower ping locations from Spencer Hartford's phone over the night in question that you sent in your last email.'

'Let me guess, he was in Canberra the whole time I asked?'

'Right on. A residential address near the city centre. Sorry I couldn't be of any more help.'

'No. That's perfect thanks, Hattie. Completely rules him out as a suspect. It's always good to have confirmation.'

'Okay. I will see you soon, yeah?'

Nick liked the young tech analyst. She was great at her job. 'I will try. Got to go. Bye.'

'Who was that?' Joanna asked.

'Hattie Boyd. She's the homicide squad's resident tech analyst. A very handy part of our team,' he replied.

'Where's she from? What's that accent?'

Nick shrugged. 'Eastern European. I'm not entirely sure.'

Nick indicated towards the port and headed down to the Hartford residence. He turned into the street and pulled up out front of the house. There was no red coupe out the front, and no black Mercedes in the driveway.

'Looks like no-one is home,' Joanna said. 'Maybe he's made a run for it?'

Nick shook his head. 'No chance. He knows he didn't kill Emily, and he'll think we are nowhere with the Mattazio case.

Too much time has passed. He'll think he's got us over a barrel. He'll be itching for a battle.'

They pulled into the driveway and walked up to the front door. Joanna knocked, and they both stood and waited. He pulled out his phone and dialled his number. 'No answer,' he said after it rang out.

'What next? And what are we going to do about Cook?'

Nick scratched at the stubble on his chin and grinned. 'How good is this, though? We've got two to go after. Don't worry about Cook. The chief will find him. Let's deal with Spencer first.'

They turned back out and made their way towards the main street again. Joanna had the great idea that maybe Spencer was at the law firm of Nigel Stratton, and they decided to head there to take a look.

The carpark was small, and he parked his unmarked police car beside a navy-blue Bentley. It was the only car in the carpark and Joanna commented as she got out, 'You think it's Stratton's?'

'Most likely. Not sure how many people would have three hundred-thousand-dollar cars working here.'

They walked in through the front doors, which were open, and made their way into the front reception. The building was modern and spacious, and he could see a line of glass walled offices along the right-hand side wall. He shrugged at Joanna in the empty reception entrance, and she followed him on through the door into the hallway, looking for signs of life.

'Police,' Joanna called out.

'In the back here,' said a voice from the back side of the office.

They walked down the hallway and came to the biggest office in the back corner of the building. A thin man, with a thick mane of grey hair and piercing blue eyes with black-framed glasses, sat in a big leather chair, looking blankly back at them. 'Good morning, officers,' he said with a knowing smile. He pointed to the chairs in his office. 'Please. Take a seat.'

Nick sat down first, followed by Joanna. 'Detective Sergeant Nick Vada and Senior Constable Joanna Gray,' he said to the man, knowing correct formal titles were smart speaking to lawyers. 'I'm guessing you're Nigel Stratton?'

'Your reputation proceeds you detective. I've read up about you. You don't quit, do you?'

'No. I don't. I don't like seeing people doing the wrong thing and getting away with it.'

'I can see that,' Nigel replied. 'I just can't believe it. I've been sitting here all day trying to process it since I saw the news. Emily was like a daughter to me. She met Spencer here in these very offices.' Nick could see that the old man was clearly in shock, and his eyes shone with tears. 'And now Emily's dead. And Spencer is a killer.'

Nick realised that Spencer clearly hadn't spoken to him yet then. He would've told him that he didn't kill Emily if he had, and decided to ease the lawyer's pain, only slightly. 'Spencer didn't kill Emily, Mr. Stratton. It's a lot more complicated than that.'

Nigel looked at him in shock. 'Wha, what do you mean?'

'Emily was killed by an undercover cop involved in the Griffith drug trade. He was concerned that she might expose his identity,' Joanna said.

'So, Spencer didn't do it?'

'No,' he replied. 'But he has killed someone in the past.'

Nigel looked down away from him again. 'Hmmm. That I might know a bit more about. It was never proven.'

'Linda Mattazio. We have fresh DNA evidence that ties him directly to the scene. We have an arrest warrant for him.'

Joanna's phone rang, and she looked down at it, and her eyebrows raised. 'I've got to take this,' she said to the two men as she walked out of the room.

Nick sat with the elderly lawyer and asked about a younger Spencer Hartford. Nigel told him about his time as his lawyer during the Mattazio murder, and his deep ties with the Hartford family, and the stranglehold they had on the region for over one hundred years. He spoke of moving to Edithvale, his wife's hometown, and Spencers move to the river town when he finally finished university. He spoke of how Spencer met Emily, who was a young intern still studying to become a lawyer, and their courtship here in the very walls of his offices.

Joanna walked back into the room and bent down and whispered in his ear. He sat up straighter at the news. 'Nigel. Any other ideas where we might find Spencer?'

Nigel looked down at his phone. 'No idea. But I want to help you. Would you like me to try and call him?'

Nick nodded. 'Yes, please.'

Nigel pushed his glasses up and dialled a number on his phone. After a few seconds, he answered. 'Hello Spencer.' He was quiet for a beat and then, 'Yes. Yes. I know. I know you didn't do it, son. Where are you? Let me know come to you and we can sit down and best figure out a position to take?'

He finished the call and placed the phone down on the bench with a sigh. 'He's with his new assistant. That blonde thing.' He paused. 'You know, I think they are sleeping together.'

Joanna smiled. 'We think you're right.'

'He's at the Quest Motel down near the river port. Last room at the end of the carpark.'

Chapter Thirty-Four

Miles sat in his Ute near the corner of the police station and watched Amy Davidson walk through the doors with her kid in tow. He scratched at the inside of his arm and knew he had to get away for another hit before he did something stupid.

He knew five years ago that he could've walked into that station and ran the joint, but now as he sat in the decrepit farm Ute, and came down from the drugs he had taken earlier in the day, he wondered just how far he had fallen from the decorated officer he had been when he was sent out to Griffith that first time, and knew that he couldn't go back now. He was too far gone.

The news on the radio had not stopped all day. It told him that prominent local lawyer Emily Hartford had been killed by her husband, federal politician, Spencer Hartford. His day had been made when he had first heard the news while he was parked in front of Amy Davidson's parent's house, but his mood had turned sour when he watched her walk to her car with her son. He had been watching the house for a few days now and tried to find the perfect moment to get rid of her, but she always had her kid by her side, and he may be cruel, but killing a kid was something he would never do. He followed her and started to panic, when he realised she was headed for the police station. He knew the news of Emily being killed by her husband would soon turn when Amy told them the whole story, and he knew that she knew his full name, and a quick search on any database would bring him up immediately.

Bo's death was an unfortunate one, and in normal times, he would have considered him a close mate. But he had been sloppy, and stupid. Why he had decided to come out and tell Bo the truth he still questioned, and he knew that by doing it, he had just given his new friend a death sentence. Because the truth was, he could never go back to just being a cop, this new life was just far too good. The money, the woman, the power and most of all, the drugs. He knew he was using too much, and that the family would soon find out, but knew he just had to deal with this problem at hand before he worried about the next ones.

Miles stiffened in his seat as he watched Nick Vada and another woman walk out of the front doors of the station and get into a car. What the hell was he doing here? He had known Nick many years ago, in a different time when he had worked in Sydney two stations over, and they had socialised in similar circles back then. He heard all the stories about him as a homicide detective and had seen him in and out of the news about his last few cases, and knew he was a hard bastard. He knew he would skirt the lines between right and wrong to get what he wanted, and he knew that he wouldn't stop if he was on his case here.

His phone buzzed in the centre console again and it made him pause. Chief Inspector of the drug squad, Peter Winter, was calling him directly. As he viewed the phone, he knew that then and there that his time in the police force was truly over. Peter Winter would never, ever call an undercover cop directly. Ever. He wondered what the hell he wanted. Surely they didn't know already that he had killed the lawyer? It was inconceivable; he had been as careful as he could. The hanging was a little bit more dramatic than he usually would do, but he thought with the painkillers, people would never have made a connection.

Seeing the phone call, and now seeing Nick Vada in town was enough. He needed to get out of town and wait it out until all the shit died down. He was a bushman long before he was a policeman, and he immediately thought of his old friend Porky Butcher, who lived out in the bush near the river on the outskirts of town. He would head there and wait, and when the detectives were gone, he would come back and deal with Amy once and for all. She was going to pay for going to the police. He wondered about his job back in Griffith, and checked his other phone again, surprised that Leo, his boss and godfather of the family hadn't called. He always kept close to Leo and had developed a close relationship with the elder boss. His tight relationship seemed to be the reason he was still alive. The family was notorious for using their help and then getting rid of them when the time was right, and he seemed to be one of the lucky ones. He knew that if they ever found out he was a cop, he'd be killed within a week. No matter where he was in the world, they had close ties everywhere.

Miles waited another hour until he saw that the sun was beginning to set in his rear-view mirror and did a quick U-turn and headed for the state highway. He had booked a motel room in town, but knew with the cops around potentially now looking for him that he had to get away. He thought about what he had left in the room and had to not worry about what was there. Clothes were replaceable. His freedom wasn't.

Miles wound his window down and lit his ice pipe as he drove. He thought he could wait until he got to Porky, but the pull was too strong. How he'd even gotten addicted to it was a dumb story in itself. The family had nothing to do with the ice trade, and he knew they would have gotten rid of him the minute they found out he was using, but the stuff was just way too good to quit. He held the steering wheel with his knees and twirled the lighter under the bulb as he drove in a clockwise direction. As it began to heat up into smoke, he inhaled quickly, doing his best to not lose any of the precious vapour. The relief was instant, and he felt a warm surge wash over his body. It was like a warm hug and a head massage all at the same time, and he closed his eyes for a short second and exhaled. 'Fuuuuuck,' he said as the smoke blew out the window.

The dirt track down to Porky's caravan was rough and deeply rutted, and he bumped down the beaten track in the old Ute. He found the junction where you turned down easily and cut in through the bushland. He could see glimpses of the Murray River, the water fast flowing and bubbling on its way toward the Torrumbarry Weir, as he slowed and pulled to a stop near the campsite.

Miles got out to the peaceful sound of the running river close by and kookaburras calling in the trees. Porky had lived down here ever since he was a kid, and when his father had died, he had lived down here as a teenager while he decided what he was going to do with his life. He hadn't seen Porky in a few years since he had been undercover and he knew as soon as he saw him, he would understand. Porky was an old crook from way back, and had a deep distrust in the law, which was one of the main reasons he decided to live a life on the land. He had once told him he was the only copper in his life he hadn't punched on the spot, and he assumed he'd be pretty proud to hear his time in the force was done.

'You're still no fuckin' good at sneaking,' Porky said from behind him.

He jumped and spun around, with the life scared out of him. 'Jesus, you scared the living shit out of me.'

Porky stood leaning against a gum tree with a hunting rifle pointed towards the ground. He couldn't have weighed more than 50 kilograms, and his arms were covered in old green and purple faded tattoos from his time in prison. He was a Vietnam veteran, and one of smartest bushman he had ever seen in his life. He was completely self sufficient and extremely paranoid about the outside public. He smiled at Miles, and Miles could see some more of his top row of teeth had fallen out.

'Been a long time, young fella.'

Miles laughed and walked over and gave him a big hug. He could feel the bones in his chest and shoulders as he hugged him, and for the first time in his life he felt that the once immortal bushman, may be soon meeting his maker. 'I'm sorry it's been so long, mate. If you had a bloody phone, I woulda' called you every day.'

Porky scoffed. 'What, and get brain cancer? No, thank you.'

He looked around. 'Hasn't changed since I was here last.'

'Nup'. And why would it? I got everything I need right here.' Porky looked at the young man up close. His once strong and muscular frame was thin, and his eyes were darting around, assessing for dangers that weren't there. He could see scabs on the inside of his left arm and his usually always clean-shaven face was lined with stubble. 'You look like shit.' He pointed at his arms. 'You using? What are you on?'

Miles looked down at his arm and placed it behind his back. 'Nothin' Just a little something to help take the edge off.'

Porky was a reformed heroin addict from back in his time in Vietnam and could see a user from a mile away. 'If you're here to get away from that shit. You're in the right place,' he said.

Miles shook his head. 'I'm not. I'm in big, big trouble, Porky. I need a place to lie low.'

Porky smiled. 'You still a copper?'

Miles shrugged. 'Not for much longer.'

'Well then. You've come to the right place.'

Chapter Thirty-Five

Nick and Joanna headed for the Quest Motel as Joanna ran through her phone conversation with Lisa Hartford. Spencer's sister had been in London now for over twenty years and hadn't spoken with her brother or any other family members for that whole time.

She had never planned on calling Joanna back until she started her Saturday morning by opening her laptop and looking at the Australian news like she always did. Her mouth nearly hit the floor when she saw her own brother's face, staring back at her with multiple photos. She read through every story as fast as she could and felt sick to her stomach. She could've stopped this years ago, but chose to stay silent, and in doing so, had aided in the early end of another woman's life.

She found the message from the police officer from a few days earlier and listened to it much more intently this time.

She hadn't heard from the Australian police in all these years after the murder of Linda Mattazio, and couldn't believe it had taken them so long to find her to talk to about the case again. Those hot summer nights when she was sixteen played through her head like a movie throughout her life over and over, and as she sat looking at the news articles, it began again from the beginning, as clear as the days when it first happened.

The summer night, when on their way home from a family dinner, Spencer had seen Linda with her friends and had stopped and berated her in front of everyone. She had never, ever seen her brother so angry, and had never known he had such a mean jealous streak. She guessed that maybe their relationship after that night had ended because she was nearly never spoken of again after that night, and the second memory she had of him from that summer was the one that had shaped the rest of her life.

She remembered her mum and dad being in Sydney for a function. And Spencer promising his mother he wouldn't leave the farmhouse and would look after her for the weekend. She remembered watching the taillights of his Ute exiting their farm. And she remembered the Ute coming back, and seeing Spencer standing in the garage with a dead look on his face she had never seen before and would never see again. She remembered his missing boot and wondering where it was, and the tone he had used with her in the darkness.

When she saw the news a few weeks later that the body of a young woman had been found, only a half hours drive away from their farm, which was soon confirmed to be that of missing woman Linda Mattazio, she felt like her life would never been the same. She knew that he had done it the minute she saw Linda's face on the TV. And knew from that point on that her relationship with her brother was over, and she could never trust him again.

She rang the number and spoke with the woman detective and outlined every single piece of information that she could remember from those two nights. As she spoke, it was like a weight had been removed from her chest, and she felt for the first time in her life that she could finally breathe, and she thought that maybe, just maybe, Linda Mattazio's family could finally find some peace. The detective was kind and caring and thanked her for the information. She asked if it came to it, would she be willing to testify? To put her brother away for good? Which she agreed. Enough was enough. One woman killed was more than enough, and now he had killed again. She could no longer stand idly by.

Nick once again thanked Joanna for her good work as he turned into the carpark of the Quest Motel. They immediately sighted Spencer's black Mercedes and Victoria's red couple at the far end of the carpark. 'That wasn't as hard as I thought it would be,' Joanna said.

They pulled in beside the Mercedes and got out. He didn't predict it would be a difficult arrest. He knew that trying to find Miles Cook was going to be the tough one, and the one he needed more than anything. He needed to catch him and prove to Bec that he did the right thing. He walked to the door and politely knocked. 'Police.'

Nick heard the rattle of the chain, and the click of the door lock as the door opened inward, to reveal Victoria standing in the opening, wearing black workout leggings and a white singlet. He struggled to take his eyes off the beautiful women, and he wondered whether it was just the way the world worked these days. All the pretty women seemed to be attracted to the worst men. 'I was just about to come down and see you, detective,' she said.

'You were?' he replied.

Victoria looked over at Spencer, who sat at the end of the dining table in the room behind a laptop and was smiling with a look of triumph on his face. 'I was,' she replied. 'I was coming down to tell you that the night Emily passed, Spencer was with me the entire time. I even have some video I would be happy to show you.'

His brain was telling him he would love to see that footage, but he had matters much more pressing at the current time. 'Keep your footage please, Victoria,' Joanna replied. 'We're not here for that.'

Spencer looked curiously in Joanna's direction. 'Well, what are you here for then?'

Joanna looked at Nick and smiled. 'Can I?'

'Be my guest.'

Joanna walked in his direction. 'Spencer Hartford. You are under the arrest for the murder of Linda Mattazio. You have the right to remain silent. Anything you say or do could be used against you in the court of law. You have the right to an attorney, and if you cannot afford one, one will be provided to you by the New South Wales government.'

She pulled him up off his seat and placed his hands in handcuffs. Spencer's look of triumph had slightly diminished, but he still looked like he thought he was one step ahead. 'You're wasting your time. I had nothing to do with it.'

Joanna replied from behind him. 'We've been speaking with your sister.'

The triumphant smile on Spencer's face flickered and then vanished as he looked at his assistant. 'Victoria. Call Nigel,' he said.

'I don't think he'll be much help,' Nick said matter-of-factly.

The trip back to the police station was a sombre one, and they could almost hear the cogs in Spencer's brain working in overdrive, trying to figure out a way to get out of the situation that he was in. Nick had done this drive many times over the years and knew the feeling Joanna would be having in the passenger seat. The feeling of winning. Of triumph. It was the best feeling he had ever had as a detective. That your gut feelings were right, but he didn't feel it at that moment. He knew he was right, but it was a hollow victory. He opened his phone again to check for any calls or messages from Bec and found none. He knew what he had done was the right thing to do. But he struggled to believe it could be at the expense of his entire relationship with her. She was his grounding. His moral compass when he needed advice, and he had had to do the complete opposite this time and go against her wishes. But he knew it was the right thing to do.

They arrived at the police station, which had now turned into a media frenzy. Media vans lined each side of the streets with their satellite dishes pointed to the sky. A crowd was milling near the entrance doors, ready for the perfect moment, the perfect photo. And Nick was ready to give it to them.

Spencer spoke for the first time since the motel room. His final request. 'Can we please go through the back entrance? I didn't do it. This'll be the end of my career.'

Nick didn't even turn back. 'Nope. I think your face all over our TVs is just what we want tonight, isn't Joanna?'

'It is,' she said with a devilish grin, still facing forward.

Chapter Thirty-Six

The booking of Spencer Hartford was surprisingly smoother than Nick had thought it would have been. Nigel Stratton was no-where to be seen, and Spencer had clamped up the minute that it was explained that his legal counsel he had asked for had denied his request to represent him. Satisfied that for now there was nothing further they could do for the day with Spencer, he left Joanna with another of the Edithvale detectives, and headed for Greg Baseley's office once again for counsel.

Greg hung his phone up and waved him in. 'Bloody great work. You found him quicker than I thought.'

'He's not the one I'm worried about. What are we going to do about Cook?'

Greg sighed. 'Hmm. I've been worried about that, too. I looked him up. He's from here, you know?'

Nick nodded. 'I did. I've met him a couple of times back in the day. He was a good fella back then. Can't say that now, though. He's obviously involved in some bad business.'

'Agreed. Well, sounds like you'll be the best person to find him if he's still around here. I've put the feelers out around town, see if there's anyone that remembered him from back in the day. But I don't like our chances.'

Nick could feel the feeling again. The tingle on his tongue, the itch at the back of his throat. He needed to get out of here before Joanna found him again. 'Good work. I'm sure someone will find something. I'm going to go and see Bec, make a few calls, see whether I can find something myself.'

'Good luck with that,' Greg said. 'Chat later.'

Nick headed out of the back entrance and made his way on foot to where he knew was the nearest pub, the Caledonia Hotel. It was an old workman's pub, and when the Edithvale Hotel had undergone massive renovations, the old crowd of day drinkers, bar flies and workmen had moved on to another old girl, not happy with the sweeping changes. As he walked, he thought of Miles Cook, and his time working around him back when he was on the beat. He remembered back to the last time he had seen him, just like he remembered it when he saw Miles' face on that computer monitor again after so many years.

Nick had just been made a Senior Constable and was enjoying the fruits of a decent pay rise that he had sorely needed. He had met Miles out at the pub with some other officers having drinks between stations and had hit it off with him when he had told him he was from Edithvale after he had mentioned Milford. The two men had enjoyed a night on the drink and had even made acquaintance with two women in the pub that were in the city for a netball trip. It had been a great night and a good bonding experience with a fellow cop, but unluckily, he had never seen him again except for one more time.

About eight months later, he had been in the midst of messy breakup number twenty in his life, or at least that's how it felt when he sat at the bar alone, on his day off at three in the afternoon. He had been in since the bar had opened, and the publican, knowing who he was, had let him continue to drink despite just how drunk he was becoming for the time in the day. He knew he had night shift starting at seven and decided he better get home and try and sober up before he headed in. It had become like an art to him, to see just how drunk he could get before he could sober up again and be better than every other cop in the building. But little did he know, he had pushed himself a little too hard this time.

Nick waved off the publican's request to call him a cab and struggled to walk to his Ute parked in the back corner of the car park. He only lived four blocks away from the pub, but the station was a fair drive, and he wasn't going to try and grab a lift from anyone else. He knew he could make it home; he had done it a million times before.

Nick started his Ute and tilted the sunshade mirror down to show his face. He looked like shit. His eyes were bloodshot, and his face was beetroot red. No matter, he thought, a cold shower and a couple of hours' sleep and he'd be back fighting fit.

Nick looked across the carpark which was still quite empty. He wondered why and then realised it was a Monday afternoon. He felt guilty, but knew the drinking was the only way he could push through all of the bad thoughts in his head. He idled forward, wound the windows down and slapped his cheeks twice to wake himself up, and then indicated out of the carpark.

The streets were busy with school traffic, and he slowed to a grid lock of SUVs parked trying to get into the school entrance near where he lived. When he finally got through the gridlock, he accelerated harder than he would've liked and felt the wheels spin rather uncharacteristically for his old four-wheel drive. He tried to focus on the next intersection, which was only one block from home, and began to feel like he was in the clear, until he heard the 'whoop whoop,' of a police siren directly behind him.

Nick struggled to make out the model through the rear vision mirror and prayed it was one of his own, and potentially one of the younger constables he'd been training up. He knew a smile and abit of praise could get him out of anything, but when the door opened, he read 'COO23,' on the door, which meant it was from the Coogee station from a few suburbs over. And he knew he may be in some serious trouble.

Nick watched as an officer walked beside his Ute and slowly came to his side window. As his face came into view, he realised it was Miles Cook and he hoped that his one fun night with his equal would be enough to get him out of what could potentially be the end of his career.

'Nick! Mate! Sorry, didn't know it was you,' Miles said with a smile.

He tried his best to act as sober as possible. 'Hey Miles. How are ya' mate?'

'Good mate, good. Hey, listen, did you know you back taillight is out?'

He did, and couldn't believe a blown bulb could put him in the situation he was in. 'Shit really? Nah, didn't know. Sorry mate, I'll get it fixed as soon as I'm home, yeah?'

Miles slapped the side of the door and laughed. 'Course mate, no dramas.' He pulled out the breathalyser and plugged a clear plastic tube into it. 'Just gotta' do a random breath test. Standard procedure, Nick, you know how it is.'

Nick looked at the machine with fear. 'Hey listen, Miles. I had a massive night last night, had a birthday party. I might still be a little over.'

Miles's brow furrowed. 'Weren't you working? Albert Smith said he dropped some paperwork off to you last night, said you were shift supervisor?'

Nick stiffened in his seat and tried to back track. 'Ah, yeah. I was, I mean..'

Miles sensed his apprehension. 'Just blow here, Nick. I'm sure you'll be fine.'

Nick leant forward and blew into the machine until it sharply beeped. 'Stop,' Miles said.

The sunlight shone from behind Miles, and he struggled in the light to see his face. He kept both of his hands on the steering wheel and distinctly remembered the Grinspoon song that was playing on the radio, while another cop had his career in his hands.

Miles placed his right hand inside the Ute with the machine, which read 0.10. He felt his shoulders slump, and he breathed out as he saw the numbers and knew he was done for. In the next beat, Miles's thumb moved to the clear button, and he held it for 3 seconds, clearing the reading. He leant down and his face was blocked by the sunlight, and Nick finally saw his whole face. 'How far off home are you?'

Nick pointed to the next block. 'Red fence on the next street,' he said.

'You owe me,' he replied as he stood back up and tapped on his door. 'Have a good day.'

It was the last time they had met as policemen.

Chapter Thirty-Seven

The Caledonia was near derelict, and his mind was cast back to the tired façade of his own old local pub in Milford, the Coachman's Inn. The columns around the once grand veranda were filled with cracks, and in various sections, metal props wrapped in builders caution tape held up sections of the structure.

The lineup of cars in the park out the front made Nick smile. Old Toyota Hilux's, Commodores and rough Falcons were the pick of this crowd, and he knew he'd feel at home here. He looked around as he got to the entrance and the guilt of having his first drink in months was starting before he'd even tasted it. But he knew it had to be done. His thirst was unquenchable. He needed alcohol in his system to think; it was how he best operated.

Nick walked through the saloon doors and looked at the scene before him. The bar was close to the front windows, which were all open, and invited a cool breeze into the building. The crowd was rough, which was just the way he liked it. He knew there would be no judgement here. He walked up to the bar, and a young woman stood chatting to a couple beside him. She looked at him, and then did a double take. He was used to it these days. With his face on TV and in the papers so much, a lot of people had started to recognise him more and more.

'You look familiar. Have we met?' The young bartender said in his direction with a smile.

'Nah, I get it a lot. I've got a familiar face,' he replied. 'Just a schooner of Great Northern, please.'

The bartender walked over and grabbed the frosty glass from the fridge, and then flicked the tap towards her and poured a near perfect beer. He was almost drooling at the prospect of the amber liquid, and his hand was shaking as he grabbed the glass off the bar.

The bartender's eyebrows raised. 'That'll be $5.'

Nick tipped the beer down and immediately felt the relief and buzz as the alcohol hit his system. He felt like a warm blanket had wrapped around him and welcomed him home. If

Bec didn't want him, he knew he'd be quite happy to just stay alone. The beer was better company half the time anyway. He picked the glass up and moved toward the far table in the front corner of the bar. He didn't need anyone recognising him sitting up in the main bar. He sat down and opened his phone again. Same as earlier, no calls or messages. He was just as stubborn as Bec and wasn't going to admit defeat. He was right, and she was wrong; it was as simple as that. He sipped the last half of his glass in quiet contemplation and noticed an older man with a limp walk in. The man ordered a glass of beer and a packet of salt and vinegar chips from the bar and then walked over in his direction.

Nick did his best to not attract attention and did the tried and tested technique of looking at his phone to show he didn't want to be bothered. The man seemed to ignore it and walked in his direction. 'Seat taken, young fella?' he asked.

Nick admitted defeat and pointed at the seat across from him. 'Nah.'

The man cracked open the pink packet of salt and vinegar chips and ripped the packet in half, sliding it into the centre of the table. 'You want some?'

His stomach rumbled and as he drained the dregs of his first beer, he knew he couldn't resist; they were his favourites after all. 'Thanks.'

The old man wore a light blue terry towelling bucket hat and had a stained and tired blue singlet on. He looked like he had lived a hard life, and Nick had fond memories of many men like him from his youth. He sipped from his beer and munched on the chips, and looked at Nick with a keen eye. As he swallowed his last mouthful, he asked, 'What's got you down, young fella?'

Nick tore at the beer coaster on the table. 'Nothing. Women,' he said finally.

The old man scoffed. 'Can't live with em', can't live without em'.' He held his hand out over the table. 'Pete Sandlehurst.'

'Nick.'

'You from around here, Nick?' Pete asked.

'Milford.'

Pete sipped his beer. 'Great little spot. Good fishing too. What do you do for work?'

Nick was a good judge of character, and knew the way the conversation would go when he said it, but thought Pete seemed like a nice enough bloke. 'Detective,' he replied.

Pete smiled. 'You're a copper? Shoulda' picked it. I was one myself many moons ago. Worked out Darlington Point way. I guess our kind are attracted to each other, aren't they?'

'I guess so,' he said.

Nick excused himself and grabbed him and Pete a fresh beer. He returned to the table and slid the glass in his direction. 'For the chips.'

Pete gave him a toast. 'You're too kind.' And then sipped from the new beer. 'You here to put our old mayor away?'

'Something like that. It's a bit more complicated.'

'Want some advice?'

'Sure.'

Pete sipped from the beer again. 'Trust your gut. It never failed me in my time on the job.'

His phone vibrated in his pocket, and he felt a rush of relief, hoping it was Bec finally caving. But as he read the screen, he saw it was Joanna.

'Hey Jo.'

'Nick, where are you?'

Nick paused for a beat, and then realised if Joanna was going to be his partner for real, she needed to know everything, all of his flaws. 'I'm at the Caledonia Hotel having a beer. Just behind the police station.'

There was a pause at the end of the line and then she replied, 'Okay. If that's what you need right now, I'm not going to tell you off. But get this, remember Jason Peters, the detective we spoke to about your mother's case a few years back? I called him, thought he might have heard of Miles or might know something, and he reckons he might have a lead. Can you get back to the station?'

Nick liked the way she asked. Can you get back to the station? Very political, and gave him one of two options. Fight or flee. He sculled his new beer and burped. 'Yep. Give us five, I'll be back.' He hung up his phone and made to stand when Pete smiled and said, 'I still remember like it was yesterday. The rush. Everything is the most important thing in the world.' He shook his head. 'I don't miss it for a minute.'

Nick placed a ten-dollar note on the table and, feeling rejuvenated from Joanna's call replied, 'And the minute I feel that way, I'll stop. But for now, next rounds on me. I'm off.'

Nick made it back to the station quickly and seamlessly blended into the small team that had congregated in the squad room. The beer had made him feel whole again, and the slight buzz of alcohol was what he knew he needed to make his head straight. After a round of introductions and small talk with Jason Peters, the legendary detective, Nick sat in the squad room with a team of around ten other officers beside Joanna and listened to Greg Baseley speak.

Greg stood up at a small lectern beside a whiteboard. 'Alright. Things are moving quickly here, so I need you all to keep up.' He pointed to the high-definition image on the whiteboard, the still taken from the camera in the Hartford backyard. 'This is Sergeant Miles Cook. He is an active member of the N.S.W police narcotics division and is currently deep undercover. He has managed to embed himself with the Matriana crime family in Griffith, one of the toughest and most ruthless Italian cartels in Australia. We have an arrest warrant active for him for the murder of Emily Hartford, a local lawyer here, and wife of our friend in cell five, Spencer Hartford.' The room was full of murmurs and chuckles, and Greg held his hand up for quiet. 'Settle down. We've put some feelers out, but it was our good friend here from Milford.' Greg pointed out Joanna. 'Senior Constable Gray here, that had the brilliant idea of asking our friend

Jason Peters, who is a long-serving member of our team and knows this town and its inhabitants back to front for help.'

Joanna gave a meek wave and smile as Nick moved up beside her. 'Good thinking.'

Joanna gave him the side eye, and he knew exactly what it meant; I know what you've been up to, and I covered for your ass, and you owe me. 'Thanks,' she said.

Jason Peters walked up to the lectern and cleared his throat. 'Hi all, I'm sure you all know who I am. And if you don't, ask your dads. I'm the old timer around here, and I know a fair bit about this town and its past inhabitants.' He pointed to the photo of Miles and then a map of what looked to Nick like the Murray River. 'Miles Cook grew up here in Edithvale and had a rough childhood. Beaten and abused by his father, his mother ran out on them both when he was young. I remember personally bringing him in as a kid for the odd misdemeanour. Anyway, his dad was a real piece of work, and ended up dying when Miles was a teenager, which left Miles out on his own.' Greg, beside him, taped another photo up beside Miles of a different face. One Nick had never seen.

'This is Porky Butcher,' Jason continued. 'He's an old school bushman, been in the same spot, a camp site out near

Torrumbarry Weir on the river for many years. Honestly, he hasn't caused us any trouble in the last ten years. But he was a real mean piece of work back in my younger days when he got back from the Vietnam war, and I've heard a story or two about him. And one that I know is true is that Porky took Miles in as a teen and Miles lived with him for his formative years before he joined the force.'

As Jason continued talking, Nick ruminated on the information about Miles' childhood and wasn't surprised. Miles always came off to him in his first few meetings as a little rougher than the rest, and it's what drew him to him in the first place. His upbringing sounded hard. To be treated that way by both of his parents, and then brought up by someone who had experienced their own trauma, it was much harder than anything he had gone through, and he almost felt sorry for him.

Greg was back up in front of everyone and started talking. 'Now we believe he's holed up here with Porky Butcher. Our last known location from his police device was this spot, and we believe he could be armed. Now our plan is for Detective Sergeant Vada and Senior Constable Gray to approach first, and we are hoping to use Nick's past relationship to draw him out. Now we are under strict instructions to not shoot. I repeat, do not shoot. He must be taken in alive. If he runs, we'll catch him. I'm sure of it.'

One of the officers put their hand up. 'What about Porky?' she asked.

Greg nodded. 'Good question, Constable Oaks. Yes, we must be prepared for Porky to potentially try and show us force. He's been in the bush a long time, and has a deep mistrust of the government and us after his years after the war. I never want any casualties in a high-profile operation like this. But if he shoots our way, we must show force.'

Nick felt Joanna stiffen beside him. He remembered the feeling of being shot in the shoulder, and he was sure Joanna remembered dragging him to an ambulance back at that time. His shoulder still ached from time to time and had never felt right since. He wasn't prepared to go through that again. He was going to be careful.

Chapter Thirty-Eight

Miles sat on the deckchair with a broken base and sipped on a warm bottle of beer. As the sun rose, he realised he was running out of gear, and he could feel his skin beginning to crawl at the prospect of coming down.

He had smashed his police phone when Porky had found it the night before, and he had thought he was going to kill him. Porky still hadn't calmed down the next morning, and walked past him muttering to himself about satellites and drones. He knew they could track him to this spot, but assumed he'd still be a few steps in front. He just needed some time to think.

Porky had spent the night sorting his gun collection and ammunition, and had a bad feeling about Miles' arrival and seeing his phone on him. The bloke was clearly a heavy drug user, and had changed from the young larrikin he had brought up in his caravan. He wanted to do right by him but was starting to feel paranoid that with him around, his days might be numbered, and he knew he had to be prepared. The sky was clear blue, and the sun was already beginning to heat the ground up around them, and he assumed that if the police were going to come, they'd do it at night, when the men were both supposedly asleep. He'd let Miles sleep for the first night, but he was feeling the effects now of a full night on watch, and needed him to help out if they were to be prepared.

By the time Nick and Joanna reached the turnoff, it was mid-afternoon, and Nick could feel the nervous energy in the air. He could tell Joanna was feeling the pressure, and he wanted to assure her everything was going to be okay. He placed his hand on her knee quickly. 'Hey listen. Remember when I got shot?'

She turned to him. 'Yeah. Like it was yesterday. I've been thinking about it all day.'

He chuckled. 'Me too. And I'm not going to let that happen to me again, alright? The minute we feel any trouble, we are turning around and leaving, okay? I'm too old for a gunfight.'

Joanna seemed appeased. 'Okay. Thanks. I just don't want to see you hurt again.'

'Me either,' he said. 'Whose idea was it to look for his phone location?'

Joanna continued looking ahead. 'Me. I called your friend Hattie. She got it within five minutes.'

Nick smiled. He knew she'd make a great detective. 'That's great work, Jo. Honestly.'

He watched the map on his phone and found they were near the pin drop that Porky's campsite was supposedly at. He could see a small break in the dense gum trees off to the right which headed down in the direction of the river, and he parked his car in the table drain and switched off the ignition. Behind him, there were two more police vehicles in tow, and they parked higher up the road behind them.

They both got out and grabbed their black bulletproof flak jackets and put them on. Joanna was used to the bulk, but he struggled to get his comfortable, as they weren't standard uniform when he was on the streets, and he'd barely ever worn one. They both checked their sidearms for ammunition one last time, and Joanna tapped him on the shoulder. 'Look.' She pointed high up in the gumtree at the far side of the break in the tree line. A surveillance camera sat above, pointed directly down at their car. He turned to the group in the cars behind them who were gearing up too and pointed at the

camera in the tree and gave them the hold signal. He wanted
to go at this alone first, and then see what happened from
there.

Nick looked at the M4 carbine semi-automatic rifle sitting
in the base of his weapons locker in his boot. They were
standard issue for the riot and public protection squad, and
the chief inspector had managed to get ten through a special
order. Just in case weapons, he called them. He leant into the
boot and pulled the matte black rifle out into the sunlight. It
was a menacing-looking weapon, with a thick black scope on
the top and a long-protruded magazine that formed the front
handle. He clicked the slide back and forward and felt the heft
of it in his hands. It was used more as a show of force than an
actual weapon, and he'd never used it in the field before.

Joanna's eyebrows raised at his weapon of choice. 'Is that
really necessary? I thought you said you don't want to get
into a gun fight?'

'This is more than a gun. This is a conversation ender.' He
pointed up at the camera. 'I'd like to think the minute they
see this; they surrender.'

'Let's hope,' Joanna replied.

Nick walked to the edge of the driveway and looked back
at the Edithvale crew, who were all in position, champing at

the bit for some action. He hoped it wouldn't come to that as they crept slowly down the driveway, which was nothing more than two four-wheel-drive tyre tracks, deeply rutted and full of potholes. The centre was so high that a standard car wouldn't have made it more than a few metres. He led and Joanna followed him cautiously until they came to a large, felled tree log that ran alongside the track near the river. They slowly inched up behind the log, and he popped his head over to survey the scene before them.

There was an old caravan which looked to have not moved in many years, and beside it was an old hut made of railway sleepers and rusted corrugated iron. In front of the buildings was a campfire, which had an array of cooking utensils around it, along with logs on each side to sit. On any other day, it would have been a nice place to enjoy a beer. But today was not that day. He needed to find Miles. He needed closure. And he needed to show Bec that he was right, and that Emily didn't die for nothing.

'What do you see?' Joanna asked.

Nick bent back down. 'Campsite. Caravan and a hut. Can't see anyone yet.'

'What do you think?'

He opened his mouth, but the words were drowned out by the log in front of them exploding in a hail of gunfire. He heard the pop, pop, pop of a rifle from down below and he screamed at Joanna, 'Stay down!' He threw his body between hers and the log and wrapped his arms around her. He could feel her trembling in fear and cursed at himself. He'd had a bad feeling about this plan from the minute Greg Baseley had outlined it. They should've just waited Miles out and not try and bring him out of a place where the owner was clearly paranoid about law enforcement.

'What the hell are we going to do?!' Joanna yelled.

Nick looked down the driveway along the thick tree cover, which went down towards the caravan. He didn't know what the Edithvale team would be thinking behind him, but knew he could rely on Joanna. He handed her the M4 rifle. 'See this button on the side?' He pointed at the small clip next to the trigger. 'Safety. Flick it before you fire. And tuck it hard into your shoulder. It has a hell of a kick.'

Joanna looked down. He could tell she was scared, but her gaze was still, and she looked up at him, defiant. 'What do I need to do?'

Nick pointed over the log. 'Cover fire. I don't care where you shoot. Just shoot. They'll retreat when they hear that thing going off.'

Nick turned to leave, and Joanna grabbed him on the shoulder. 'Good luck. Please don't do anything stupid.'

Nick winked. 'You either.'

Down in a crouching stance, he got to the end of the log. He turned to Joanna and gave her a nod, and he watched as she moved the compact rifle up and over the log. The noise of the rifle shots was deafening in the quiet bush as she began to hammer the tree line above the campsite in a spray of bullets. He ran as hard as he could along the tree line and made it to the opening at the edge of the campsite without any bullets heading his way. He slowed and backed into a small corrugated iron building he assumed was an outhouse as the loud gunfire receded.

'Police!' he yelled. 'Miles. If you're here, come out with your hands up! We don't want any trouble. Surrender now and walk away, mate.'

Nick heard the voice, which sounded like was coming from the caravan. 'Is that you Nick?'

It was Miles' voice. He recognised it immediately. 'It is. Miles, please. Don't do this. Come out with your hands up and let's end this.'

There was silence, and then Miles spoke. 'Okay. I'm coming out.'

'Don't you fucking dare, Miles!' came a husky voice from further away. 'Don't give the bastards the satisfaction!'

Nick assumed this was Porky. He had guessed with a campsite as run down as this that the camera high in the tree was not operational. Over half of the cameras set up in Australia were, so he took a calculated risk. 'Miles, you're completely surrounded. We've got the whole special operations team all up in that tree line. Would you rather come with me or deal with them? If that's Porky here with you, please tell him we're not here for him. He's free to walk away.'

Nick tucked his sidearm in the back of his pants and held his hands up. He walked out from behind the shed into the opening. 'Don't shoot. I'm unarmed.'

Nick walked to the campfire with his hands up, and felt that if he was going to die, now was probably the closest he had ever been in his life. He could feel his heart beating in his chest and his hands trembled as he waited for the next bullet that was sure to hit him. He stopped at the campfire and turned to the caravan. 'It's just me, Miles. Come out.'

Footsteps came from the caravan and a head bent down under the low door opening and emerged. Miles Cook stood before him, a shadow of the confident young man that he had remembered. He was still tall, but his once muscular frame was emancipated, he guessed from what looked like heavy drug use. His eyes darted nervously up along the tree line, and he scratched the inside of his arm. His face was pale now, and he had a rough-looking beard that looked like he hadn't trimmed in months.

He looked at Nick and smiled. 'Long time.'

'Too long,' Nick replied. 'Mate, you know why I'm here. I've got to take you in.'

Miles shook his head. 'You can't. I'm dead, mate. I'm dead. If I'm locked up, they'll get me in there, you know that.'

Nick shrugged. 'We don't.'

From his peripheral in the old shack, he just caught the sight of the gun barrel as it rose up out of the window frame. He jumped away from the fire and reached for his sidearm in the split second, sure he was about to meet his maker. Miles must have seen it too because he heard him yell, 'Porky! Don't!'

Nick heard multiple shots at once, from the tree line and the shed, and when the noise went away, he lay in the hard dirt on his side, with his gun pointed at Miles. He couldn't feel anything, and quickly glanced down. No bullets holes. What a relief, he thought. He watched Miles, who had got up quickly and ran towards the shack. 'Don't move Miles!' he yelled, but Miles had already got through the door frame.

Nick stood up and waved in Joanna's direction up in the tree line. It was a wave of thanks. I'm alive. He then slowly crept with his pistol pointed to the ground towards the shack. It was only one room, and as he made the door, he heard muffled cries inside. 'Don't shoot,' came the voice from inside. He stepped into the shack and looked at the scene in front of him. Miles sat on the floor with his legs spread out, cradling an old man's head. The man who he assumed was Porky Butcher was rail-thin and wore jeans that hung on his frame. He wore a faded and torn blue work shirt which, from the top pocket to the collar, was covered in blood. He spluttered, and blood came from his mouth.

'Help him,' Miles said, as his voice broke.

Nick watched in silence at the old man's ragged breathing as he breathed his last few breaths. 'There's nothing we can do for him, Miles.'

As he spoke, Porky's body fell still, and his eyes remained open.

'Nooooo!' Miles wailed. 'Fuck, no!'

Nick stood quietly as Miles wiped his face and breathed in and out. 'I know it's hard, Miles. But you need to come with me.'

Miles placed Porky's head gently on the floor and stood up. Nick could see his pistol still in his hands and he raised his up to Miles' centre mass. 'Put the gun down, mate.'

Miles' face was one of resignation. 'Just shoot me, Nick. I extended you a kindness once. I looked after you, mate. Just do it, I'm dead already.'

'You don't know that. Please, put the gun down.'

Nick watched Miles' blood-soaked hand that held the pistol and prayed that he didn't have to go through with what he thought was about to happen next. Miles' hand moved, and as his pistol came up quickly in his direction, he had no choice. He fired twice, hitting Miles in the centre of his chest, and Miles stepped back, almost in shock, as blood spluttered from his mouth, and fell to the floor.

Chapter Thirty-Nine

Miles was in a critical condition, but Nick had managed to drag his body out of the campsite and up the driveway towards the waiting group, who had watched on in awe at his bravery. They had raced him back to the state highway, where he was picked up by an air ambulance in handcuffs. He would live. But would spend the rest of his life in prison, under prisoner protection. And in constant fear of retribution once the Matriana family found out his true secret. He was not wanted by anyone in this life; the police had discarded him, and the family would soon, too. It was more than he deserved for ripping Emily's life away from her while she was still so young.

Nick and Joanna returned to the Edithvale police station as heroes, with rounds of applause from all sides. As the sun set,

Greg Baseley got a constable to go and grab a slab of beers and everyone stuck around to celebrate the arrest.

Greg ushered him away for a quiet chat in his office, and he sat down at his desk with a grin from ear to ear. 'Bloody great work, mate. You got him.'

Nick knew Greg was right, but it felt like another hollow victory. An innocent civilian had died during the gun fight, and he felt terrible for the death of Porky Butcher. 'We did,' he replied. 'But at what cost?'

Greg sipped from his beer and sighed. 'Yes. That was unfortunate.'

'More than unfortunate. That old fella didn't need to die.'

'That's the risk he was willing to take when you shoot at the police. He knew the consequences.'

Nick sipped from his beer. He had taken two bottles to the bathroom, sculled the first bottle, and threw it in the waste bin before starting on his second. It felt good to be drinking again. 'I guess.'

Greg's phone rang on the bench, and he picked it up. 'Hello. Hey Mark, give us a sec.' He placed the receiver back in the cradle and pressed loudspeaker. 'You're on.'

'Nick, you not answering your phone these days?'

Nick pulled his phone out of his pocket again, and was surprised to see three missed calls, all from the chief. For someone who had been desperate to see a notification, he wasn't sure how he missed them. 'Sorry chief. It's been abit crazy here.'

'No dramas, son. Just wanted to call and congratulate you on your fine work. Greg tells me you put your neck on the line, which you didn't need to, and you got results. Again.'

Nick leaned closer to the receiver. 'Can you wait a sec, chief?'

'Sure,' the chief replied.

Nick got up and walked out of the office over to Joanna, who was laughing and chatting with two other officers. 'Hey, got a sec?'

She looked at him with a smile. 'Of course.'

Nick walked her back into the office and sat her down in the chair beside his. 'Sorry chief, had to get the real star of the moment in, Senior Constable Gray.'

'Joanna, you were my next call. How are you holding up?'

Joanna's smile from the squad room was more subdued in Greg's office. 'I'm okay, thank you. Am I in any trouble?'

Greg and the chief laughed simultaneously. 'Not at all, senior constable,' the chief replied. 'Classic case of self-defence. You were being fired upon, and you defended yourself.'

'And saved my skin in the process,' Nick replied.

Joanna sat a little straighter in her chair. 'Okay. I'm just sorry we had to do what we did.'

'What you did was apprehend a killer of women, senior constable. And a man who was causing chaos in the inner rankings of the narcotics division in our police force. Now. I would like to ask another question. How would you like to come and work for us? And become a detective for real? I think Detective Sergeant Vada would like a partner. God knows I haven't found one yet who he'll keep.'

Joanna looked in Nick's direction when she replied, 'I'd like that. But I have one small request.'

'What's that?' the chief asked.

'That either you or Inspector Baseley speak up the chain to get the team in Milford more help. We are critically understaffed, sir. And me leaving isn't going to help that anymore.'

Greg wrote some notes on his desk. 'I can sort that, Mark.'

'Good work. Now you two celebrate the win. And I will see you both back in Sydney by the end of the week. Joanna, we will arrange accommodations for you for the time being while you sort the move. And great work again. Both of you.'

The line went dead, and Greg Baseley held his beer out in a toast to the duo. 'Congratulations on your promotion, detective.'

***

Two days later, Nick stood in the disabled toilet beside the church and swigged from the hip flask he had bought the minute he had got back into town after the shoot-out. He believed the drink had saved his life, that small amount enough to calm his nerves in a dangerous situation, and to empower him to run towards potential death.

Nick walked into the chapel; and stood near the back row with Joanna beside him. Filling the row were members of the Edithvale police force who had known Emily personally and, from what he could see, there wasn't a dry eye in the house. He looked further ahead through the sea of people to find Bec, and spotted her in the front row, with her mother and father beside her.

His feeling of triumph when he had returned to the station with Joanna, to cheat death, and to come back alive felt empty, when he had checked his phone when they had returned. Nothing. No calls. No messages. He had sat later that night in the motel room with the adrenaline of the shoot-out finally gone in the silence, and tried his best to formulate a text to Bec that would give her the closure he was sure she needed.

'Arrested Miles Cook. Undercover police officer. He murdered Emily, Bec. She can now truly rest in peace.'

He had re-written the last line over and over, and though the way it was written looked the best. It was the ending they needed. He had made a mistake, but he had righted it. He was sure she would see what he had done, and would love him even more for it.

Back at the funeral, he hadn't had a reply, and he itched in anticipation for the reception back at Emily's home. He was going to finally get a chance to talk to Bec and tell her just how sorry he was. The service was a quiet affair, and Emily's eulogy was completed by her mother. He was surprised Bec hadn't got up to say anything, but knew just how hurt she was by it all. He just wished he could walk up to her, and hold her in his arms, and make everything all okay again.

The service ended, and Joanna drove his car in silence towards the Hartford home. The weather was overcast, like mother nature knew that grieving was on the cards for the day, and as Joanna turned into the street the Hartford's home was on, she finally broke the silence.

'Bit odd having the wake here, don't you think?'

Nick agreed. He wondered whose idea it was. The beautiful Hartford home was now going to be empty. 'I thought the same. I'll ask Bec whose idea it was when we get there.'

Joanna glanced across at her new partner. His eyes were blood shot, and he looked to have not shaved in the past few days. His shirt was crinkled, and his hair was longer than when she first met him. She knew he was back drinking and had spied him sipping from a silver hip flask outside the church in the morning. It was something she was going to have to keep an eye out for.

'How's that all going?' she asked.

'Haven't spoken in a few days now.' He looked down at his hands. 'I don't know.'

She patted him on the shoulder. 'It'll be alright. Whatever will be, will be.'

Chapter Forty

The street out front of the Hartford home was full to the brim with cars, and Joanna navigated a tight reverse parallel park near the far end of the block. They got out together and Nick walked around behind the car to the footpath.

Joanna looked at him with a sad smile. 'You look terrible. Flatten your hair and tuck your shirt in.'

Nick did what he was told and straightened up his posture. 'What are you, my mother?' He held his arms out. 'How's that?'

'Better,' she replied.

Inside, the home was full to the brim, and the pair navigated the long hallway into the open section where the living and dining area were. Joanna headed off in the direction of the sandwiches and he headed towards the row of eskies, which were sitting in front of the kitchen island bench. He grabbed a beer and walked over into the lounge room to sit down on the couch and looked around the beautiful house once again. He felt sick that poor Emily didn't get the chance to live a full life and enjoy the beautiful home into old age. Even if they hadn't arrested Spencer for the murder, he imagined a life where she left Spencer, possibly met someone new, and enjoyed a long and healthy life in the old home.

'Nick?' said a voice from behind him.

Nick turned and saw Bec's father, Ram, standing beside the couch. He held a beer in his hand and asked, 'Can I sit?'

'Of course, mate.'

Ram sat down across from Nick and sipped from his beer. 'How are you?' he asked.

Nick shrugged. 'As good as I can be. Getting shot at wasn't on my bingo card this week.'

'Yes. We had Greg Baseley over at our motel room this morning. He came and told Bec and me the whole story. You're lucky to be alive.'

'I guess.' Nick pointed behind him. 'I've got Joanna to thank for all of that. She saved my skin.' He waited a beat and mustered the courage to ask. 'How's Bec? Is she here?'

Ram nodded and pointed towards the back garden. 'She is. I think she's outside.' Ram paused, as if trying to formulate the words. 'I'm not sure what's going on between you two, but I've put in the good word for you as much as I can. You're a good man, Nick.'

'Thank you, Ram,' he replied. 'I'm going to head out for a chat.'

Ram smiled. 'Good luck.'

Nick walked out through the back sliding doors, making the same walk he had done the first time he had come to the home to see Spencer, and eyed the beautiful gardens once again. Everything was still pristine, and the pool looked more inviting than ever. He looked down the rolling green grass to the Oak tree and saw Bec sitting on the cast iron bench seat underneath it, with Remi the bulldog beside her.

Nick sipped from his beer and mentally prepared himself. He knew that she just needed time, that everything would be okay again. He walked down the grass in her direction, and she looked up from her phone.

'You look terrible,' she said.

Nick chuckled. 'You're not the first person to say that today. Can I sit down?'

She nodded, and he sat beside her. Remi moved across the bench and jumped up into his lap happily and he scratched under her chin. 'Hello girl. What's going to happen to her?' he asked.

Bec moved her hand over and patted her head. 'She's coming home with me.' She pointed to his beer bottle. 'Drinking again?'

'Just a couple today. Nothing serious.'

'Hmm.'

Nick placed the bottle down beside the chair and turned to her. She looked beautiful in her black dress and muted makeup. Her dark eyeliner accentuated her shining brown eyes, and he wanted more than ever to just hold her. He took a deep breath and then spoke. 'I just wanted to say that I'm sorry. I know you wanted me to leave it. But I didn't. And I got the answers we needed.'

Bec turned to him, and he could see the shining tears in her eyes. 'That's just it, Nick. I didn't need answers. I don't care what happened. I lost my best friend. And nothing will ever bring her back. Whether she hung herself up there.' She pointed to the branch directly above her. 'Or whether someone else did it. I honestly don't care.'

Nick sat and looked at her, and couldn't understand what she was thinking. He had solved it. He had got the answers. What more could she want? He opened his mouth and then closed it, trying to formulate what to say.

'I don't know what to say, Bec. This is my job. This is my life. I get results.'

Bec placed her hand on his shoulder. 'I know. And I'll never be able to change that. Your job is your life. And I'll always be number two.'

Nick stopped. 'Wait. No. That's not what I meant.'

She had a sad smile. 'It's exactly what you meant, Nick. I love you. I will always love you. But we are done.' She wiped the tears from her eyes and tried not to ruin her makeup. 'I'm sorry.' She leant in and gave him a short kiss and held him. He wrapped his arms around her and felt hot, wet tears streaking down his face. It was over. She knew it, and he knew it.

Bec stood up and walked up toward the back deck to where most of the funeral goers had congregated. Remi gave him one last look as well and set off for Bec on the deck. He stayed underneath the Oak tree in silence and felt empty. Dead inside. He had no-one. And there was nothing he could do to fix it. His job was his life.

His phone rang, and he pulled it from his pocket and answered. 'Chief. How are you?'

'Good. How was the funeral?'

'Like all funerals. Sad.'

'How's Bec?'

'Let's not talk about that,' he replied.

'Understood.'

'What did you need?' he asked.

The chief cleared his throat. 'I know it's not great timing. But we've got another job. Murdered backpacker last year and now we've got another missing. In Secret. Far north of the state.'

'Secret?' he asked.

The chief laughed. 'Yeah. Funny name for a town. Population of twenty.'

Nick grabbed his beer from beside the bench seat and drank from it. The alcohol fizzed in his throat and his body and mind felt clear again. This was his life. He was a detective, and he was put on this earth to bring closure for families. And to put bad people away.

'No dramas. I'll head that way tomorrow.'

'You sure? You don't need a break?'

It was the last thing on his mind. He needed to work. 'Nah, I'm right. Chat soon.'

Nick ended the call and sat in the silence in the beautiful garden. He was on the move again, to the other end of the state, to solve another mystery, and to find more answers. That deep tired he had felt when he awoke in the morning seemed to evaporate at the thought of a new case, and he knew that every decision he had made over the past few weeks had been right.

He walked up the grass, over the deck through the crowd and into the house. He spoke shortly with Emily's parents, who were effusive in their thanks for him finding answers for them, and then he found Joanna. He wanted to get out of there before he saw Bec or her parents again. Joanna saw the look in his eyes and knew immediately he was ready to leave. She placed her plate of food on the bench and left her drink full beside it, and made her way for the exit.

Once they cleared out their rooms that afternoon, they got into the respective cars and headed for Milford, where he planned to spend a night on Warranilla, his sister Jess' farm with his baby nephew, and recharge before he headed toward the outback for his next adventure.

THE END

Thank you so much for reading my novel.

If you enjoyed The Last Sunset, make sure you check out the other books in this Nick Vada series I have been writing – Warranilla, Into The Flames, The Storm & The Kooleybuc Hotel. They are all on Amazon now.

Also, if you enjoyed my novel, please consider leaving a rating/review on my Amazon book page or on Goodreads. It means a lot to hear what my readers think as reviews are hard to come by and I personally read every review.

Jason Summers

Printed in Great Britain
by Amazon